NEW MAN IN TOWN

Another figure appeared, a tall, cadaverous alien wearing something loose, with polka dots. "I understand that you have expressed an interest in the scientific theories of probability."

"*Purely* scientific, friend. I'm a spacer by profession—an astrogator—so my interest's only natural. I'm especially intrigued by permutations and combinations of the number seventy-eight, taken three at a time. Fives are wild."

"Ah...*sabacc*." The alien took a long drag of orange smoke, exhaled softly. "I believe you could be inducted into the, er, research foundation. But first...well, a small formality: your ship name if you please, sir—strictly for identification purposes. There are certain regressive, antiscientific enemies of free inquiry—"

"—Who carry badges and blasters?" The human laughed. "*Millennium Falcon*, berth seventeen. I'm Calrissian, Lando Calrissian."

Also by L. Neil Smith
Published by Ballantine Books

The Probability Broach

The Venus Belt

Their Majesties' Bucketeers

The Nagasaki Vector

Lando Calrissian and the Mindharp of Sharu

A NOVEL BY
L. NEIL SMITH BASED ON THE CHARACTERS AND SITUATIONS CREATED BY GEORGE LUCAS

A Del Rey Book

BALLANTINE BOOKS • NEW YORK

A Del Rey Book
Published by Ballantine Books

Copyright © 1983 by Lucasfilm Ltd. (LFL)

Library of Congress Catalog Card Number: 83-90767

ISBN 0-345-31158-2

Manufactured in the United States of America

First Edition: July 1983

Cover Art by William Schmidt

This book is dedicated to
Robert Shea and Robert Anton Wilson.

PROLOGUE

"*SABACC!*"

It was unmercifully hot. Tossing his card-chips on the table, the young gambler halfheartedly collected what they'd earned him, an indifferent addition to his already indifferent profits for the evening. Something on the unspectacular order of five hundred credits.

Perhaps it was the heat. Or just his imagination.

This blasted asteroid, Oseon 2795, while closer to its sun than most, was as carefully life-supported and air-conditioned as any developed rock in the system. Still, one could almost *feel* the relentless solar flux hammering down upon its sere and withered surface, *feel* the radiation soaking through its iron-nickel substance, *feel* the unwanted energy reradiating from the walls in every room.

Especially this one.

Apparently the locals felt it, too. They'd stripped right down to shorts and shirt-sleeves after the second hand, two hours earlier, and looked fully as fatigued and grimy as the young gambler felt. He took a sip from his glass, the necessity for circumspection regarding what he drank blessedly absent for once. No nonsense here about comradely alcohol consumption. Most of them were having ice water and liking it.

Beads of moisture had condensed into a solid sheet on the container's outer surface and trickled down his wrist into his gold-braided uniform sleeve.

What a way to live! Oseon 2795 was a pocket of penury in a plutocrat's paradise. The drab mining asteroid, thrust cruelly near the furnace of furnaces, orbited through a system of pleasure resorts and vacation homes for the galaxy's superwealthy, like an itinerant junkman.

The gambler was wishing at the moment that he'd never heard of the place. That's what came of taking advice from spaceport attendants. A trickle of moisture ran down his neck into the upright collar of his semiformal uniform. Who *said* hardrock miners were always rich?

He shuffled the oversized deck once, twice, three times, twice again in listless ritual succession, passed it briefly for a perfunctory cut to the perspiring player on his right, dealt the cards around, two to a customer, and waited impatiently for the amateurs to assess their hands. Real or imagined, the heat seemed to slow everybody's mental processes.

Initial bets were added to the ante in the middle of the table. It didn't amount to a great fortune by anybody's standards—except perhaps the poverty-cautious participants in the evening's exercise in the mathematics of probability. To them the gambler was a romantic figure, a professional out-system adventurer with his own private starship and a reputation for outrageous luck. The backroom microcredit plungers were trying desperately to impress him, he realized sadly, and they were succeeding: at the present rate, he'd have to drain the charge from his electric shaver into the ship's energy storage system, just to lift off the Core-forsaken planetoid.

Having your own starship was not so much a matter of

being able to buy it in the first place (he'd won his in another *sabacc* game in the last system but one he'd visited) as being able to afford to operate it. So far, he'd lost money on the deal.

Looking down, he saw he'd dealt himself a minus-nine: Balance, plus the Two of Sabres. Not terribly promising, even at the best of times, but *sabacc* was a game of dramatic reversals, often at the turn of a single card-chip. Or even without turning it—he watched the deuce with a thrill that never staled as the face of the electronic pasteboard blurred and faded, refocused and solidified as the Seven of Staves.

That gave him a minus-four: insignificant progress, but progress nevertheless. He saw the current bet, flipping a thirty-credit token into the pot, but declined to raise.

It also meant that the original Seven of Staves, in somebody's hand or in the undealt remainder of the deck, had been transformed into something altogether different. He watched the heat-flushed faces of the players, learning nothing. Each of the seventy-eight card-chips transformed itself at random intervals, unless it lay flat on its back within the shallow interference field of the gaming table. This made for a fast-paced, nerve-wracking game.

The young gambler found it relaxing. Ordinarily.

"I'll take a card, please, Captain Calrissian." Vett Fori, the player in patched and faded denyms on the gambler's left, was the chief supervisor of the asteroid mining operation, a tiny, tough-looking individual of indeterminate age, with a surprisingly gentle smile hidden among the worry-lines. She'd been betting heavily—for that impecunious crowd, anyway—and losing steadily, all evening, as if preoccupied by more than the heat. An unlit cigar rested on the table edge beside her elbow.

"Please, call me Lando," the young gambler replied, dealing her a card-chip. "'Captain Calrissian' sounds like the one-eyed commander of a renegade Imperial dreadnought. My *Millennium Falcon*'s only a small converted freighter, and a rather elderly one at that, I'm afraid." He watched her for an indication of the card she'd taken. Nothing.

A nasal chuckle sounded from across the table. Arun Feb, the supervisor's assistant, took a card as well. There was a hole frayed in the paunch of his begrimed singlet, and dark stains under his arms. Like his superior, he was small in stature. All the miners seemed to run that way. Compactness was undoubtedly a virtue among them. He had a dark, thick, closely cropped beard and a shiny pink scalp. Drawing on a cigar of his own, he frowned as he added what he'd been dealt to the pair in his hand.

Suddenly: "Oh, for Edge's sake, I simply can't make up my mind! Can you come back to me, Captain Calrissian?" Lando groaned inwardly. This was how the entire evening had gone so far: the speaker, *Ottdefa* Osuno Whett, for all his dithering, had been the consistent big winner, perhaps owing to his tactics of continuous annoyance of the others. Fully as much a stranger in the Oseon as the young starship captain, at the moment he was operating on considerably less good will.

"I'm sorry, *Ottdefa*, you know I can't. Will you have a card or not?"

Whett assumed an expression of conspicuous concentration that might have been a big success in his university classes. *Ottdefa* was a title, something academic or scientific, Lando gathered, conferred in the Lekua System. It was the equivalent of "Professor."

Its owner was a spindly wraith, ridiculously tall, grayheaded, with a high-pitched whiny voice and a chronically indecisive manner. It had taken him twenty minutes to order a drink at the beginning of the game—and even then he'd changed his order just as the drink arrived.

Lando didn't like him.

"Oh, very well. If you insist, I'll take a card."

"Fine," Lando dealt it. Either the academic had an excellent poker face, or he was too absentminded to notice whether the resulting hand was bad or good. Lando looked to his right. "Constable Phuna?"

The squat, curly-headed tough-guy he addressed was T. Lund Phuna, local representative of law-and-order under the Administrator Senior of the Oseon. It was not, apparently, the happiest of assignments in the field. The uniform tunic hanging soddenly over the back of his chair looked nearly as worn as his companions' work clothes. He lit cigarette after cigarette with nervous, sweaty fingers, filling the cramped, already stifling room with more pollution. He wiped a perspiration-soaked tissue over his jowls.

"I'll stand. Nothing for me."

"Dealer takes a card."

It was the Idiot, worth zero. Given the circumstances, Lando felt it was altogether appropriate. If only he'd headed for the Dela System as he'd planned, instead of the Oseon. He'd seen richer pickings in refugee camps.

Bets were placed again. Vett Fori took another card, her fourth, as did her assistant, Arun Feb, asking for it around the stub of his cigar. *Ottdefa* Whett stood pat. A Master of Sabres brought the value of Lando's hand up to a positive-ten, as a final round of wagering commenced.

Arun Feb and Vett Fori both folded with a nine and minus-nine respectively. The cop Phuna hung grimly on, his broad features misted with sweat. Lando was about to resign, himself, when Whett excitedly cried, "*Sabacc!*" slapping the Mistress of Staves, the Four of Flasks, and the Six of Coins down on the worn felt tabletop.

The *Ottdefa* raked in a meager pot: "Ahh ... not exactly the Imperial Crown jewels, nor even the fabulous Treasure of Rafa, but—"

"Treasure of Rafa?" echoed Vett Fori.

She might as well ask, thought Lando, she isn't doing herself any good playing cards.

"I've heard of the Rafa System," the mine supervisor continued, "everybody has. It's the closest to our own. But I haven't heard of any treasure."

The academic cleared his throat. It was a silly, goose-honk noise. "The Treasure of Rafa—or of the Sharu, as we are now compelled to call it, not for the Rafa System, my dear, but for the ancient race who once flourished there and subsequently vanished without a trace—is a subject of some interest."

This had been delivered in Whett's best professorial tones. Vett Fori's weathered face, impassive enough when it came to playing cards, plainly displayed annoyance at being patronized. She picked up her cigar, stuck it between her teeth, and glared across the table.

"Without a trace?" Arun Feb snorted with disbelief. "I've *been* there, friend, and those ruins of your—what'd you call 'em?—'Sharu,' are the biggest hunks of engineering in the known galaxy. What's more, they cover every body in the system bigger than my thumbnail. They—"

"Are not themselves the Sharu, my dear fellow, of whom no trace remains," Whett insisted, his tone divided between pedantry and insulted reaction. "I certainly ought to know, for, until recently, I was a research anthropologist for the new governor of the Rafa System."

"What's a bureaucrat want with a tame anthropologist?" Feb asked blandly. He blew a final smoke ring, mashed his cigar out on the edge of the vacuum tray, and took a long drink of water. It dribbled down his chin, soaking the collar of his soiled shirt.

"Why, I suppose," sniffed Whett, "to familiarize himself thoroughly with all aspects of his new responsibilities. As you are no doubt aware, there is a native humanoid race in the Rafa; all of their religious practices revolve about the ruins of their legends of the long-lost Sharu. The new governor is a most conscientious fellow, most conscientious indeed."

"Yes," Lando said finally, wondering if the anthropologist was ever going to deal the next hand, "but you were speaking of treasure?"

Whett blinked. "Why, yes, yes I was." A shrewd look

came into the academic's eyes. "Have you an interest in treasure, Captain?"

More interest than I've got in this game, Lando thought. I wish I'd steered for the Dela System, no matter how much easier it is to land a spaceship on an asteroid than a full-scale planet. Soon as this farce is over, that's precisely what I'm going to do, win or lose, even if the astrogational calculations take me twenty years.

"Hasn't everybody?" Lando answered neutrally. He extracted a cigarillo from his uniform pocket and lit it. Treasure, eh? Maybe there was something to be learned here, after all.

"Not quite everybody. Speaking for myself," the scientist intoned, beginning at last to shuffle the thick seventy-eight-card deck, "my interest is purely scientific. What use have I for worldly wealth? One for you, one for you, one for you, one for you, and one for me. One for you, one for you, one for you . . ."

"Well, you surely came to the right place, then!" Vett Fori guffawed, picking up her cards. "No worldly wealth to get in your way at all! What *are* you doing here, anyway? We didn't hire any anthropologists."

Lighting another cigarette, Constable Phuna spoke bitterly. "Seeing how the other half lives, that's what! I saw his entry papers. He's studying life among the poor people of a rich system—on a fat Imperial grant, speaking of worldly wealth. We're *specimens*, and he—"

"Please, please, my dear fellow, do not be offended. I aspire only to increase our understanding of the universe. And who knows, perhaps what I learn here can make things better in the future, not just for you, but for others, as—"

Vett Fori, Arun Feb, and T. Lund Phuna spoke almost simultaneously: "Don't do us any favors!"

"Do *me* one," Lando suggested in the embarrassed silence that followed, "tell me about this treasure business. And kindly deal me a card while you're about it, will you?"

Bets were placed again and additional cards dealt out.

Lando, having actually lost interest in the increasingly slim pickings the game afforded, watched absently as the card-chips in his hand transmuted themselves from one suit and value to another. He paid a good deal more attention to what the anthropologist had to say.

"The Toka are primitive natives of the Rafa System. As Assistant Supervisor Feb has so cogently pointed out, they and the present colonial establishment co-exist among the ruins of the ancient Sharu, enormous buildings which very nearly occupy every square kilometer of the habitable planets. I'll see that, and raise a hundred credits."

Arun Feb shook his head, but tossed in a pair of fifty-credit tokens from a dwindling stake. Vett Fori folded, a look of disgust on her face. She placed her still unlighted cigar back on the table's edge.

Phuna raised another fifty. "Yeah, but the really important thing about the Rafa is the life-crystals they grow there." He fingered a tiny jewel suspended in its setting from a slim chain around his sweaty neck.

Whett nodded. "Important to you, perhaps, good Constable. It is true, the life-orchards and the crystals harvested there are the chief export product of the colony, but my interest—and what I was paid to be professionally interested *in*—were the Toka legends, especially those bearing upon the Mindharp."

Glancing at his cards, Lando saw he had a Mistress of Coins, a Three of Staves, and a Four of Sabres. He dropped the requisite number of tokens into the pot just as the Three turned into a Five of Flasks: twenty-three, but it didn't really matter; Fives were wild anyway.

"*Sabacc!*"

He gathered in the largest pot of the evening thus far. "Mindharp?" the gambler asked. "What in the name of the Core is that?"

Ottdefa Whett wrinkled his nose, passing the rest of the deck to Lando. "Oh, just a ridiculous native superstition. There is supposed to be a lost magical artifact designed to call the Sharu—with whom the Toka identify in some strange fashion—to call the Sharu back when the Toka need them. Silly, as the Toka could not possibly ever have been contemporary with a civilization millions of years in the past, any more than human beings and dinosaurs—"

"I've seen dinosaurs," Arun Feb interrupted. "On Trammis III." The gigantic reptiloids of Trammis III were famous the galaxy over, and a chuckle circulated around the table.

"I take it, however," Lando said as he shuffled and dealt the cards, then watched the bets pile up again, "that you have your own theories." Somehow the talk of treasure seemed to have loosened up the pursestrings a bit, except perhaps for Vett Fori and her assistant. The gambler took a puff of his cigarillo. "Would you mind talking about them?"

The anthropologist looked as if he wouldn't mind at all, even if requested to discourse standing barefoot on a large cake of ice while his ample gray hair were set on fire.

"Well, sir, the ruins, for all that they are ubiquitous, are impenetrable, closed completely on all sides without a sign of entryway. I daresay that all the collected treasures of a million years of advanced alien culture await the first adventurer to gain admittance. I don't mind confessing to you all that I attempted it myself on several occasions. But the ruins are not only impenetrable, they are absolutely obdurate. No known tool or energy yields so much as a smudge upon their surfaces. I'll see that, and raise five hundred. Constable?"

Grudgingly, the policeman threw in five hundred credits' worth of tokens. Lando saw the bet with mild amazement and raised it a hundred credits himself.

"*Sabacc!*"

Hmmm. Things were looking up a little. He was now ahead two thousand credits. He dealt the cards a third time, wondering what prospects for a gambler might be met in the Rafa. The idea was tempting: only a handful of straight-line lightyears to navigate across, and, if he recalled correctly, a major spaceport with good technical facilities—which to him meant landing assistance from Ground Control. The *Millennium Falcon* was completely new to him. He'd be playing cards in the Dela System this very moment if he weren't such an abysmally amateurish astrogator and ship-handler. He'd balked at the long, complicated voyage and reputedly tricky approach to a mountaintop landing field, despite well-founded rumors of rich pickings in an atmosphere friendly to his profession.

But the Rafa...

He won the third hand and a fourth, was now ahead some fifty-five hundred credits. The prospects of action seemed to be encouraging him, and he wasn't noticing the heat as much anymore.

"Oh, I say, Captain Calrissian..." It was Whett again. As the stakes mounted, the anthropologist seemed the only one whose interest in desultory conversation hadn't lagged.

"Yes?" Lando answered, shuffling and dealing the cards.

"Well, sir, I...that is, I find myself somewhat embarrassed financially at this moment. You see, I have exceeded the amount of cash I allowed myself for the evening's entertainment, and I—"

Lando sat back disappointed, drew on his cigarillo. It was too much, he reflected, to have expected to get rich off this emaciated college professor. "I move around too much to extend credit, *Ottdefa*."

"I appreciate that fully, sir, and wish to...well, how much would you consider allowing on a Class Two multiphasic robot, if one may ask?"

"One may indeed ask," the gambler replied evenly. "Thirty-seven microcredits and a used shuttle pass. I'm not in the hardware business, my dear *Ottdefa*." There was an idea, however: he could rent a pilot droid to get the ship from here to the Rafa—or wherever else he decided to go. He reconsidered. A Class Two was worth a good deal, perhaps half again the value of his spaceship. In these circumstances...

"All right, then, a kilocred—not a micro more. Take it or leave it."

The Professor looked displeased, opened his mouth to bargain Lando up, examined the determined expression on the gambler's face, and nodded. "A kilo, then. I haven't any use for the thing in any event, it was attempting to help me break into the Sharu ruins, and I—"

"Will you have a card, Supervisor Fori?" Lando interrupted.

"I'm out; this game's gotten too rich for me, and I'm on shift in fifteen minutes." Much the same was true for Arun Feb. They sat through the hand, enjoying watching somebody else lose for once.

Osuno Whett, however, bet heavily with his borrowed thousand, perhaps in an attempt to tap the gambler out. He was assisted in this by Constable Phuna. The money on the table grew and grew as Lando met their every raise, increasing the stakes himself. He wanted the game over with, one way or the other.

He'd dealt himself a Two of Sabres and a Four of Coins, taking an additional card after his two opponents had accepted them. Abruptly, the Four became a Three of Flasks, and his extra, which had been a Nine of Staves, transformed itself into the Idiot.

"*Sabacc!*" Lando cried in double triumph. To judge from the money on the table before him, and the lack of it in front of Whett and Phuna, that was the game. "Where can I pick up that droid, *Ottdefa*? I'm going to put it to work immediately as a naviga—"

"On Rafa IV, Captain. I left it in the custody of a storage-locker company, intending to sell it there or send for it—now, please don't get angry! I have here the title of an official tax assessment indicating its true value. You may take these with you, or use them to get a fair price for the robot here!"

Lando had risen, violence flitting briefly—very briefly—through his mind. That he been gulled like any amateur was his first coherent thought. That he had a small but powerful pistol secreted beneath his decorative cummerbund was his second. That he could wind up dead, or in jail, on this sweltering fistful of slag was his third.

There wasn't time for a fourth.

"Hold on there, son!" the Constable said, seizing Lando's arm. "No need for any uproar. We're all friends here." He pointed with his free hand to the papers Whett had proferred. "The *Ottdefa* here can post bond to you in the full amount of—say, what's *this*?"

Lando felt something small, round, and cool thrust up beneath his embroidered sleeve. He glanced down just as Phuna was pretending to remove it, and groaned. It was a flat, smooth-cornered disk a centimeter thick, perhaps four centimeters in diameter. He knew precisely what it was, although he'd never owned one in his life.

"A cheater!" the indignant Constable exclaimed. "He had a cheater all the time! He could change the faces of the cards to suit him any time he wanted! No wonder—"

With a feral snarl, Osuna Whett took advantage of the asteroid's minimal gravity, launching himself across the table at Lando. Just as his skinny frame was halfway to its target, a dirty denym jacket flopped over his head, followed by a knobbly set of knuckles belonging to Arun Feb's right hand. There was a dull thump of contact and a muffled squeak from the anthropologist.

"Get out of here, kid!" Feb shouted. "I saw Phuna plant the cheater on you!"

The lawman whirled on Feb, fist upraised. Apparently Vett Fori trusted her assistant's judgment—and knew how to maneuver in the absence of gravitic pull. She snatched up the nearest solid object—which happened to be the anthropologist's already battered head—and dashed it sideways against the startled cranium of the police officer. Eyes crossed, he collapsed, drifting slowly to the floor. Still holding Whett by the occipital region, Fori pried the wad of official-looking papers from the unconscious scientist's fingers.

"Take these and get your ship out of the Oseon, Lando. I'll talk sense with Phuna when he comes around. He's crooked, but he isn't crazy. Besides, in theory, he works for me."

It wasn't the first rapid exit Lando had made in his brief but eventful career. However, it was passing rare for those whose money he had taken to assist him at it. With a pang of gratitude—and the feeling he'd regret it later—he made to toss his winnings back on the table beside the insensate *Ottdefa*.

"Don't you dare!" Vett Fori growled. "You want us to think you didn't win it fair and square?" Behind her, Arun Feb tapped Phuna on the pate again with a stainless steel water carafe, *tunk*! He looked up from the pleasant occupation and nodded confirmation.

Lando grinned, waved a wordless farewell on his way out the door. Twenty minutes later, he was aboard the *Millennium Falcon*, bolting down a very hastily rented pilot droid. Ten minutes after that, he was above the plane of the ecliptic, blasting out of the Oseon System and headed for the Rafa. It was the last place Whett would look for him.

He told himself.

ONE

GOLD-BRAIDED FLIGHT CAP CAREFULLY ADJUSTED TO A rakish angle, a freshly suave and debonair Captain Lando Calrissian bounded down the boarding ramp of the ultra-lightspeed freighter *Millennium Falcon*—and cracked his forehead painfully on the hatchcoaming.

"Ouch! By the Eternal!" Staggered, he glanced discreetly around, making sure no one had seen him, and sighed. Now what the deuce *was* it Ground Control had wanted him to look at?

They'd put it rather ungenteelly...

"What's that garbage on your thrust-intermix cowling, Em Falcon, over?"

Well, it *had* been something they could say without insulting references to the amateurish way he'd skidded, setting her down on the Teguta Lusat tarmac. Atmospheric entry hadn't been anything to brag about, either. Gambler he may have been, scoundrel perhaps, and what he *preferred* thinking of as "con *artiste*."

But ship-handler he was definitely not.

He frowned, reminded of that rental pilot droid he'd wasted a substantial deposit on, back in the Oseon. Let 'em try to collect the rest of *that* bill!

Stepping—gingerly this time—around the hydraulic ramp lifter, he backed away from under the smallish cargo vessel (which invariably reminded him of a bloated horseshoe magnet), shading his eyes with one hand.

Intermix cowling . . . intermix cowling . . . now where in the name of Chaos would you find—

"Yeek!"

The noise had come from Lando, not the hideous leathery excrescence that had attached itself to his ship. It merely flapped and fluttered grotesquely, glaring down at him with malevolent yellow eyes as it scrabbled feebly at the hull, unaccustomed to the gravity of Rafa IV.

Two hideous leathery excrescences!

Four!

Lando pelted back up the ramp, slamming the Emergency Close lever and continuing to the cockpit. The right-hand seat was temporarily missing, in its place bolted the glittering and useless Class Five pilot droid, its monitor lights blinking idiotically.

"Good evening, ladies and gentlemen," the robot smirked, despite the daylight pouring through the vision screens from outside, "and welcome aboard the pleasure yacht *Arleen*, now in interstellar transit from Antipose IX to—"

The young gambler snarled with frustration, slapped the pilot's OFF switch, and threw himself into the left acceleration couch, just as one of the disgusting alien parasites began suckering its way across the windscreen, fang corrosives clouding the transparency.

"Ground Control? I say, Ground Control! What the devil *are* these things?"

A long, empty pause. Then Lando remembered: "Oh, yes . . . *over!*"

"They're mynocks, you simpering groundlubber! You're

supposed to shake them off in orbit! Now you've violated planetary quarantine, and you'll have to take care of it yourself: nobody's gonna dirty his—"

With a growl of his own, Lando punched the squelch button. If they weren't going to help him, he could do without their advice. Mynocks...ah, yes: tough, omnivorous creatures, capable of withstanding the rigors of hard vacuum and Absolute temperatures. They were the rats of space, attaching themselves to unwary ships, usually in some asteroid belt.

The Oseon System was nothing *but* asteroids!

Hitching a ride from sun to sun, planet to planet, mynocks typically—

Good grief! He jumped up, banging his head again, this time on the overhead throttle board—*stupid place to put it!*—and made quick, if clumsy progress aft to the engine area. He'd just remembered something else he'd read or heard about mynocks: subjected to planet-sized gravity, they collapsed, dying rapidly . . .

After reproducing.

In a locker, he found a vacuum-tight worksuit, also scrounged up a steamhose and couplings. Shucking into the greasy plastic outfit—a pang of regret: he was ruining his mauve velvoid semiformals!—he ratcheted the steamline to a reactor let-off, cranked open the topside airlock, and, trailing hose, clambered out onto the hull.

A mynock waited greedily for him, altered by the unavoidable rumble of the hatch cover, its spore sacs shiny and distended. It was ugly, perhaps a meter across, winged like a bat, tailed (if that was the proper word for it) like a stingray, poison-toothed like a—

"Yeek!" The mynock, this time.

It floundered toward him, dragging itself along by a ventral sucker-disk. The only thing uglier than mynocks, Lando thought, were the larvae they spawned on planet surfaces. He leaped as it flicked a clawed wingtip at him, his awkwardness aboard ship bred more of unfamiliarity in a new environment than any native lack of agility. He twisted the hose nozzle, spraying the monster with superheated vapor from the *Falcon*'s thermal-exchange system.

It screamed and writhed, flesh melting away to expose the cartilage it used instead of bones. This, too, reduced quickly, washed down the curved surface of the ship, leaving nothing but gelatinous slime steaming on the spaceport asphalt.

A noise behind him.

Side vision impaired by the suit, Lando whirled just in time to ram the nozzle into a second mynock's gaping maw. It swelled and burst. Fastidiously, he played steam over himself to remove the dissolving organic detritus, then stalked grimly forward, finally destroying seven of the sickening things in all.

"Good going, Ace!" Teguta Lusat Ground Control sneered through his helmet receiver as he wiggled back through the upper airlock hatchway. *"Didn't you get an instruction booklet when you sent your nox-tops in for that pile of junk you're flying? Over."*

Pile of junk?

The only pile of junk in the neighborhood, thought Lando, sweating in his bulky armor as he cranked the hatch back down and stowed the steamlines, was that brainless rent-a-bot up forward. Hmmm. That gave him an idea.

"Hello, Ground Control," he warbled pleasantly from the cockpit only seconds after worming back out of the plastic vac-suit. "I'll have you know that this stout little vessel's often made the run to your overrated mudball in record-breaking time."

Once *upon* a time. At least that's what her former owner claimed, trying to bid up the battered freighter's pot value in a *sabacc* game he was losing badly. Lando's rented droid had failed miserably to coax anything near the advertised velocities out of the ship.

Probably some trick to it.

"By the way," Lando continued, "I seem to have the

knack of handling this baby now. Would anyone care to purchase a practically new pilot droid? Over?"

"We've heard that one before, Millennium Eff. That rental outfit in the Oseon may not maintain offices here, but they've got treaty rights. You'll have to send it back fast-freight. Expensive. Over and out."

It wasn't quite as bad as he'd expected.

Lando shipped the droid back slow-freight, balancing the extra rental time against the transportation costs. Evening had begun to fall before he'd taken care of that, *plus* all of the complicated official paperwork attendant upon grounding an interstellar spacecraft anywhere the word "civilized" is considered complimentary.

Tonight, he'd relax.

He needed it, after traveling with that confounded robot. Get a feel for the territory—by which he meant identifying potential marks, locating those social gatherings that others foolishly regarded as games of chance.

Tomorrow, he'd take care of business.

The Rafa System was famous for three things: its "life-crystals"; the peculiar orchards from which they were harvested; and what might have been called "ruins" if the colossal monuments left by the Sharu hadn't remained in such excellent repair.

The crystals were nothing special—as long as you regarded quadrupling human life expectancy "nothing special." Varying from pinhead to fist-sized, their mere presence near the body was said to enhance intelligence (or stave off senility) and to have some odd effect on dreaming.

They could be cultivated only on the eleven planets, assorted moons, and any other rocks that offered sufficient atmosphere and warmth, of the Rafa System.

The life-orchards themselves were nearly as famous— after the manner of guillotines, disintegration chambers, nerve racks, and electric chairs. It was not the sort of agriculture amenable to automation—the crystals were harvestable only under the most debilitating and menial of conditions. However, the operation was attractive financially because it came with its own built-in sources of cheap labor, two, to be exact: the subhuman natives of the Rafa, plus the criminal and political refuse of a million other systems.

The Rafa was, among its other distinctive features, a penal colony where a life sentence meant certain death.

That much was known by every schoolchild in civilized space—at least that minority with an unhealthily precocious bent for unwholesome trivia, Lando reflected as he secured the *Falcon* for the night. He strolled across the still-warm asphalt to the fence-field surrounding the spaceport, intending to catch public transport into Teguta Lusat, capital settlement of the system-wide colony.

An old, old man dressed only in what appeared to be a tattered loin-cloth, hunched over a pushbroom at the margin of the tarmac. He looked up dully for a moment as Lando strode by, then back at the ground, and resumed pushing dead leaves and bits of gravel around to no apparent purpose.

Slanting sunset caught odd angles of the multicolored alien architecture that constituted foreground, background, and horizon everywhere one cared to look on this planet. Pyramids, cubes, cylinders, spheres, ovoids, each surface was a different brilliant hue. The least of the monumental structures was vastly larger than the greatest built by living beings anywhere in the known galaxy. What passed for a town lay wedged uncomfortably into the narrow spaces between them.

Under a scattering of stars, Lando stepped lightly aboard the open-sided hoverbus, arrayed in his second-best blue satyn uniform trousers, bloused over Bantha-hide knee boots. He wore a soft white broad-sleeved tunic, dark velvoid vest. Tucked into his stylish cummerbund was enough universal credit to get him into a semihealthy table game—and the tiny five-charge stingbeam that was all the weapon he ordinarily allowed himself. Those who carried bigger guns tended, in Lando's brief but highly observant experience, to think with *them* instead of their brains.

Alone aboard the transport, he leaned back on the outward-facing bench, unsure whether he enjoyed the unique scenery or not. Traffic was a modest trickle of wheels, hovercraft, repulsor-lifted speeders. Not a few pedestrians clumped along the quaint and phony boardwalks that fronted the human buildings, and among them Lando spotted many more like the old man at the port. Perhaps they were old prisoners who had served out their sentences. The bus wheezed into the center of Teguta Lusat. Lando paid the droid at the tiller, dismounted, and stretched his legs.

The colony was an anthill built on soil scrapings in the cracks between ancient, artificial mountains. Whatever effort had been invested decorating the place (and it didn't amount to much), it remained drab by comparison with the polychrome towers surrounding it. Streets were narrow, angling oddly. Human-scale homes, offices, and storefronts merely fringed the feet of titanic nonhuman walls.

Lando walked into the least scruffy-looking bar. The usual crowd was there.

"Looking for a cargo, Captain?"

The mechanical innkeeper of the Spaceman's Rest polished a glass. Bottles and other containers from a hundred cultures gleamed softly in the subdued lighting. A smattering of patrons—not very many: it was the dinner hour and Four was mostly a family planet—filled the unpretentious establishment with an equally subdued burble of unintelligibility.

Lando shook his head.

"Too bad, Captain, what else can I do for you?"

"Anything that burns," Lando said, childishly pleased to be recognizable as a spaceman. He was puzzled, however, over the robot's commercial pessimism. This was a healthy, thriving colony, with enormous and growing export statistics. "*Retsa*, if you've got it."

In one dark corner, what might have been the same underclothed old man leaned on the same old pushbroom.

"Coming up, Captain." Deft manuevering with glassware followed.

Lando turned his back, put elbows on the bar, inquired over his shoulder: "Where could a fellow find some action around here?" He'd put it in a colonial accent—when in hick city, act hickier than the hicks. Civilized polish scares money away. "I just got in from the Oseon; my evening's free."

"How free?" The machine's optic regarded Lando appraisingly. "There's Rosie's Joint, down the street. Has a real nice revue. Just turn left at the big red neon—"

Lando shook his head. "Later, maybe. Perhaps a game— *sabacc*? Folks back home used to say I was pretty good."

Cynicism in its voice, if not upon its unyielding features, the automaton put on a show of thinking deeply. "Well, sir, I don't know . . ."

Lando offered twice the going price for *retsa*.

"I *might* know of a game—my memory stacks just aren't what they used to be, though, and . . ."

Lando placed another bill in the bar-top. "Will this cover having them recharged?"

The bill seemed to evaporate.

"Don't go away, Captain. Make yourself comfortable. I'll be right back."

The 'tender vanished almost as impressively as had Lando's money.

TWO

THE FLEDGLING STARSHIP OWNER/OPERATOR HAD scarcely picked up his drink, selected a dark, heavy, quasi-wood table, and seated himself, carefully adjusting the creases in his trousers, when another figure appeared, a tall, cadaverous, nearly human individual wearing something loose, with polka dots.

They clashed badly with his mottled orange complexion.

"Allow me to introduce myself, sir: I am the proprietor of this establishment." The creature stroked its moustaches—two separate levels filling the inhumanly broad space between nose and upper lip—took a chair to the gambler's left, and lit a long green cigarette. The young gambler noticed with amusement that the fellow hadn't really introduced himself at all.

"I understand," said the alien, "that you have expressed an interest in the scientific theories regarding the phenomenon of probability."

Lando had wondered how the subject would be broached.

He settled back with a grin, assuming the facade, once again, of an overconfident colonial, put his feet up on the chair opposite, and winked knowingly.

"*Purely* scientific, friend. I'm a spacer by profession, an astrogator, so my interest's only natural. I'm especially intrigued by permutations and combinations of the number seventy-eight, taken two at a time. Fives are wild."

"Ah . . . *sabacc*." The owner took a long drag of orange smoke, exhaled softly. "I believe you could be inducted into the, er, research foundation practically instantaneously." He paused, as if embarrassed. "But first, Captain . . . well, a small formality: your ship name if you please, sir, strictly for identification purposes. There are certain regressive, antiscientific enemies of free inquiry—"

"Who carry badges and blasters?" He laughed. "*Millennium Falcon*, berth seventeen. I'm Calrissian, Lando Calrissian."

The proprietor consulted a data-link display on his oddly jointed wrist. "A pleasure, Captain Calrissian. And your credit, I observe, is more than sufficient to support this, er, research program of ours. If you will follow me."

It's the same the galaxy over, Lando thought. A small back room, emerald-color dramskin tabletop, low-hanging lamp, smoke-filled atmosphere. In an honest game, there was a modest house percentage, and the cops were all paid off—that routine of the tavern owner's had merely been a chance to check Lando's credit rating. Only the particular mingling of smoke odors varied from system to system, and that not as much as might be expected. He might be out of his depth at the controls of a starship. For that matter, he didn't know very much about asteroid mining or needlepoint. But here—wherever "here" happened to be—he was at home.

He took his place at the table.

There were three other players, and a tiny handful of spectators currently more interested in their drinks and breathing down each other's necks than the game. He placed a few creds on the firm green surface. Card-chips were dealt around. He received the Ace of Sabres, the Four of Flasks, and Endurance—which counted as a minus-eight.

That made eleven.

"One," said Lando neutrally. He drew a Seven of Staves, which promptly flickered and became the Commander of Coins.

Twenty-three.

"*Sabacc*! Dear me, beginner's luck?" He allowed excitement to tinge his voice as he raked in the small pile of money, accepting the deck and dealing.

He carefully lost the next three hands.

It wasn't easy. He'd had to dump two perfect twenty-threes and might have drawn to a third if he hadn't stood pat with a fourteen-point hand, praying that the card-chips would keep the faces they'd begun with.

The local talent thought they had a live one.

In a manner of speaking, they were right—but not in any manner of speaking they'd find pleasant or profitable. It was one of those evenings when the young gambler felt *made* of luck, filled to the brim with spinning electrons and subnuclear fire. He ran the pot up gradually, so as not to frighten the others, conspicuously losing on the low bets, making steady, quiet gains.

Drinks flowed freely, compliments of the polka-dotted proprietor. This may have been a spaceman's bar, but at least two of the players were townies, likely splitting with the boss what they skinned from visiting sailors. The same glass of *retsa* Lando had begun with, diluted now with ice he kept having added, stood sweating on the plastic table-edging near his elbow.

"*Sabacc*," breathed Lando, flipping the trio of card-chips face upward. It was a classic: the Idiot's Array, lead-card worth the zero printed on it, plus a Two of Staves and a Three of Sabres—an automatic twenty-three.

"That cleans out my tubes," grunted the player opposite

Lando, a dough-faced anonymous little entity with slightly purplish skin. Like the gambler, he wore the uniform of a starship officer. Despite the coolness of the evening, there was a fine sheen of perspiration across his forehead. "Unless I can interest you in a small cargo of life-crystals."

Lando shook his head, adjusted an embroidered cuff. First a beat-up freighter, then a robot he hadn't even had time to inspect, now a holdful of trouble with the local authorities.

"Sorry, old fellow, but it's cash on the tabletop or nothing. Business is business—and *sabacc* is *sabacc*."

Born of fatigue, this partial transformation from rough-edged (if preternaturally fortunate) amateur into no-nonsense professional startled at least one of Lando's opponents, a stalky, asymmetrical vegetable sentient from a system whose name the young gambler couldn't quite recall. It placed three broad leaflike hands on the table—Lando thought the contrasting shades of green looked perfectly terrible together—and garbled through an electronic synthesizer fastened to its knobbly stem.

"Awrr, Captainshipness, being a sports!" It turned a petal-fringed face toward the small technician. *"Negatordly give these person ill considerations. Cargo of value, inarguability."*

The third player, a hard-bitten bleached blonde with a thumb-sized oval life-crystal dangling from a chain around her wattled neck, hooted agreement.

"Sure, Phyll," Lando replied, ingoring the woman. "Is that how you obtained that marvelous translator you're wearing—in lieu of credits in a *sabacc* game?"

The plant-being shivered with surprise. *"How thou understanding these?"*

"With considerable difficulty."

He paused, thinking it over, however. To a gambler, particularly one who was both reasonably honest and consistently successful, good will represented an important stock in trade.

"Oh, very well, Chaos take me! But only this once, understood?"

The amorphous-featured fellow nodded enthusiastically; he lasted only two more hands. On his way out the door, he reached into a pocket of his coveralls, presented Lando with a bill of lading and a few associated documents.

"You'll find the shipment at the port. Thanks for the game. You're a real sport, Cap'n Calrissian, honest to Entropy, you are."

Lando, now some seventeen thousand credits ahead, and ready to bow out of the game as gracefully as he could—or as firmly as he must—scarcely heard the little nonentity. He had blessedly near the price of the *Millennium Falcon*, right there on the table before him. A *plague* on interstellar freight-hauling! Let somebody *else* worry over landing permits and cargo manifests. He was a *gambler*!

It sure beat scraping mynocks off a starship hull!

Shortly after midnight, strolling the few boardwalked blocks toward the modest luxury of Teguta Lusat's "finest hotel"—the droid bartender's recommendation—Lando kept one hand on the credits in his pocket, the other on his little gun. It didn't seem to be *that* kind of town, still, there were *that* kind of people everywhere you went.

Beside him shambled the weirdest apparition of the mechanical subspecies he had ever seen—or even wanted to.

"Vuffi Raa, Master, Class Two Multiphasic Robot, at your service!"

The transport station with its dozens of storage lockers had been on Lando's way to the hotel. Desiring an early start on the morning's business, the gambler had thought it a good idea to pick up the droid he'd won immediately. Now he wasn't sure.

Some things are better faced in daylight.

It stood perhaps a meter tall, about level with Lando's hip pocket—hard to judge, as it could prop its five tentacles at various angles, achieving various heights. It was the shape of an attenuated starfish with sinuous manipulators—which served both as arms and legs—seamed to a dinner-plate-size pentagonal torso decorated with a single, softly glowing many-faceted deep red eye. The whole assemblage was done up in jointed, glittering, highly polished chromium.

Utterly tasteless, Lando thought.

"Most people," he had observed, watching the thing unfold itself from the rental locker, "have forgotten that 'droid' is short for 'android,' meaning *manlike*." It stretched its long, metallically striated limbs almost like a living being, carefully examined the tips of its delicately tapered tentacles. "And what kind of name is that for a robot, anyway: 'Vuffi Raa'? Aren't you supposed to have a number?"

It regarded him obliquely as they squeezed past a geriatric janitor and left the terminal through automatic glass doors, headed up the boardwalk.

"It *is* a number, Master, in the system where I was manufactured—in the precise image of my creators.

"I wish I could recall exactly where that is: you see, I was prematurely activated in my shipping carton in a freight hold during a deep-space pirate attack. This seems to have had a bad effect on certain of my programmed memories."

Wonderful, thought Lando, keying open his hotel room. A ship he couldn't fly, and now a robot with amnesia. What had he done to deserve this kind of—never mind, he didn't want to know!

The Hotel Sharu wasn't much, but it was regarded locally as the best, and he had certain standards to uphold with what he thought of as his public. He mused: in this age of wide-ranging exploration, it was entirely possible for a commodity such as Vuffi Raa to change hands many times, be bought, sold, resold, won, or lost, winding up half a galaxy away in a culture totally unknown where the product had originated.

Or vice versa, as seemed to be the case here. He couldn't recall any sapient species shaped even remotely like Vuffi Raa. Somehow, he hoped he'd *never* run across them. In any event, he thought, that'll make *two* white elephants for sale in the morning.

He'd already come to a decision about the *Millennium Falcon*.

Table talk during the *sabacc* game had been understandably sparse, but one thing was obvious even before he'd accepted those crystals for cash. The life-orchards operated on a combination of unskilled labor supplied mostly by the near-mindless natives of the Rafa—he wondered if he'd see any of the creatures while he was there, but came to the same decision about that that he had concerning Vuffi Raa's manufacturers—and supervision by offworld prisoners. The whole enterprise was a monopoly of the colonial government.

As nearly as Lando could determine, consignments of life-crystals traveled only via the Brother-In-Law Shipping Company (whatever its local equivalent was actually called), and free-lance haulers were simply out of luck. There would be no cargo for the dashing Captain Lando to *write* manifests on.

Well, that suited him. He'd trade off the cargo tomorrow.

Door-field humming securely, and the bed turning itself down with cybernetic hospitality, Lando undressed, carefully supervising the closet's handling of his clothing. Vuffi Raa offered its services as a valet, the appropriate skills being well within the capacities of its Class Two architecture, which supposedly approached human levels of intellectual and emotional response.

But Lando declined.

"I haven't had servants for a very, very long time indeed, my fine feathered droid, and I don't intend starting again with you. I'm afraid you're to change hands once more, first thing in the morning. Nothing personal, but get used to it."

The robot bobbed silent acknowledgment, found an unoccupied corner of the room, and lapsed into the semi-activation that in automata simulates sleep, its scarlet eye-glow growing fainter but not altogether dimming out.

Lando stretched on the bed, thoughts of ancient treasure dancing through his head. Of course, he considered, life-crystals weren't the only possible cargo he could take away from this place. The ancient ruins were supposedly impenetrable, but whatever race had built them, it hadn't stinted on strewing the system with more portable artifacts. Museums might be interested—and possibly in the crude statuettes and hand-tools fashioned by the savage natives, as well. High technology past and primitive present: quite a fascinating contrast.

But the treasure...

Come to think of it, there were also a few colonial manufactured goods. But that meant he'd have to chase all over the Rafa just to line up a single decent holdful—with a messy, embarrassing, and possibly dangerous takeoff and landing at each stop along the way, he reminded himself.

Of course, there was always the treasure...

No. Better stick to the original plan: find a buyer for the *Falcon.* It had been fun for a short while, but he was no real space captain, and she was far too expensive to maintain as a private yacht, even if he'd wanted one. Find somebody to give him a fair price for Vuffi Raa, as well. Perhaps the same suck—*customer.* Then ship out, tens of thousands of credits richer, on the very next commercial starliner.

He whistled the lights out, then had an afterthought. "Vuffi Raa?"

The faintest whine of servos coming back to full power. "Yes, Master?" Its eye shone in the darkness like a giant cigarette coal.

"Don't call me Master—gives me the creeps. Can you, by any chance, pilot a starship? Say, a small converted freighter?"

"Such as your *Millennium Falcon*?" A pause as the droid examined its programming. "Why, yes, er...how *should* I call you, sir?"

Lando turned over, the smug look on his face invisible

in the darkened room. "Not too loudly, Vuffi Raa, and no later than nine-hundred in the morning. Good night."

"Good night, Master."

KRAAASH!

The door-field overloaded, arced and spat as the panel itself split and hinges groaned, separating from the frame.

Lando awoke with a start, one foot on the floor, one hand reaching for the stingbeam on the nightstand before he was consciously aware of it.

Four uniformed figures, their torsos covered with flexible back-and-breast armor, helmet visors stopped down to total anonymity, stomped over the smoking remains of the door as the room lights came up of their own accord. Their body armor failed to conceal the sigil of colonial peacekeepers. They carried ugly, oversized military blasters, unholstered and pointing directly at Lando's unprotected midsection.

He removed his hand from the nighttable, hastily, but without sudden, misinterpretable movement.

"Lando Calrissian?" one of the helmeted figures demanded.

He eyed the wreckage of the door.

"Wouldn't it be embarrassing if I weren—um, on second thought, let me revise that: yes, gentlebeings, I am Captain Lando Calrissian, in the flesh and hopeful of remaining that way. Always happy to cooperate, fully and cheerfully, with the authorities. What can I do for you fellows?"

The bulbous muzzle of its weapon unwavering, the imposing armored figure stepped closer to the bed, its companions immediately filling up the space behind it.

"Master of the freighter *Millennium Falcon*, berth seventeen, Teguta Lusat Interstellar—"

"The very same. I—"

"Shut up. You are under arrest."

"That's fine, officer. Just let me get my pants—or not, if it's inconvenient. I'll be happy to answer whatever questions His Honor may wish to ask. That's my policy: the truth, the whole truth, and nothing but the truth. Support Your Local—*Umph*!"

The big cop hit Lando in the stomach with his blaster, followed it with the empty hand, balled into a mailed fist. A second figure went to work on the hapless gambler's legs. The other two swung crisply around the bed, started in on him from the other side.

"*Ow*! I said I'd go peaceably—*ghaa*! I—*unhh*! Vuffi Raa, *help me*!"

The robot cowered in its corner, manipulators trembling. Abruptly, it collapsed, curled up into a ball. Its light went out.

So did Lando's.

THREE

S<small>QUAT.</small>

Squat and ugly.

Squat and ugly and *powerful*—at least locally, Lando reminded himself with an inward groan as two of the helmeted officers dragged him into the presence of Duttes Mer, colonial governor of the Rafa.

Lando hadn't had time yet—nor the inclination—to inventory the indignities inflicted on him by the Colonial Constabulary. He seemed to be one solid, puffy bruise from neck to ankles. Avoid trouble with the cops in one system, get it in the next when you least expect it.

It hurt, rather a lot.

Yet nothing really serious had been done to him, he realized, nothing broken, nothing that would show if they ever gave him back his clothes. A thorough, workmanlike, professional beating, it had been, and, for all that it had seemed to go on and on forever, apparently a purely educational one, a few well-placed contusions meant to underline the fact that he was totally at their mercy.

He'd bloodied his own nose, stumbling against the jamb as they'd frog-marched him over the broken door of his hotel room. In hopes of not acquiring any further damage, he wished they'd put a plastic sheet under him now, to keep him from getting blood all over the governor's fancy imported carpet, the only extravagance apparent in an otherwise spare and utilitarian office.

There was a useful clue, there, if only Lando's head would begin working well enough to ferret it out.

The governor blinked. "Lando Calrissian?"

At least everybody seemed to know his name. It was a startlingly high-pitched, feeble voice, considering the ponderous bulk it issued from—and perhaps a touch more nervous, Lando thought, than current circumstances seemed to warrant. Gamblers make much more careful studies of such nuances than psychologists. They have to.

Thickly muscled, improbably broad, resembling more than anything else a deeply weathered tree-stump crowned in fine, almost feathery hair, the governor looked like the kind to play his cards close to the chest, never to take wild chances, to be a merciless, implacable player.

Turn the tables and he'd holler like a baby. Lando knew the type well.

In the present context, he felt the information wasn't terribly helpful. He glanced uncomfortably at the armored visor-wearers either side of him, then back at the governor. It doesn't matter a whit if a bully's a coward at heart—as long as he has all the guns.

The governor blinked, lifted a blocky arm, repeating the salutation—or, more likely, the accusation: "Lando Calrissian?"

"Flatten the first A a bit," Lando answered, more bravely than he felt. "A little more accent on the second syllable of the last name. Keep trying, you'll get it right."

He ran a tongue across his lips, tasted blood. His head

hurt. So did everything else. Egg-sized eyes under the silly head-thatching regarded him coldly from behind a small, uncluttered, impossibly delicate-looking desk of transparent plastic.

"Lando Calrissian, we have here a list of very serious charges against you that have been brought to our attention. Very serious charges indeed. What, if anything, have you to say for yourself?"

The governor blinked again as he finished, this time as if the very sight of Lando was painful to him. The young gambler bit back a second snappy reply. He wasn't aware of anything illegal he had done. Lately, anyway. He hadn't any qualms, particularly, about breaking the law: there were a lot of silly little planets with a lot of silly little laws. It was just that he'd rather—as an aesthetic point, mostly—be caught when he'd actually *done* something.

He decided, more or less experimentally, to add truth to the courteous obsequiousness that had failed with the cops. One never knew, the combination might work on this fat tub of—

"Sir—Your Excellency—I know nothing about any charges. To the best of my knowledge, I haven't done anything to be charged with."

He left it at that; a complaint would be carrying things too far.

The governor blinked.

Lando opened his mouth to speak. A loop of fabric from his tattered pajamas chose that moment to slip embarrassingly from his shoulder and swing. He sniffed, lifted it with whatever dignity the occasion afforded, attempted to smooth it back in place.

The governor blinked.

It was not a large room they were in. There was a wide door—but then, it was a wide governor—either side of the desk. Like the door facing the desk, through which Lando had been escorted, both were framed in plain undecorative alumabronze, the spare motif echoed in wainscotting, baseboards, and a border around the high, somehow intimidating ceiling. The pace was tinted a bilious yellow to match the governor's eyes. Instead of draperies, the windows displayed recorded scenes Lando recognized from other systems: greenish gravelly beaches, deep orange skies, scarlet vegetation. Entire *worlds* done up in bad taste.

The governor, apparently deciding Lando had been sufficiently intimidated by the longish silence, lifted a thick arm from his desk, regarded the troopers half-holding the much-abused starship captain erect.

"You are advised," Duttes Mer squeaked menacingly, "to *improve* the best of your knowledge, then, young miscreant."

Miscreant? Lando thought, did people really say *miscreant*? The governor perused a printout lying on his desk, raised downy eyebrows.

"Quite a record! Reckless landing procedures. Illegal importation of dangerous animals. Mynocks, Captain—really? Unauthorized berthing of an interstellar—"

"But, Governor!" Lando forgot himself momentarily, struggled free of the policeman on his left—then remembered where he was and clamped the astonished man's armored hand back around his elbow with a short-lived sheepish grin.

He'd realized, with a sudden, stifled gasp, that the transparent desk the governor occupied was composed entirely of gigantic, priceless life-crystals—enough to extend the life-spans of hundreds of individuals. Power, then, was the key. It explained the barren office. Money and display wouldn't impress the malevolent lump of wasted hydrocarbons sitting before him; he would be motivated only by the prospect of controlling and disposing of the lives of others.

"Sir, I had all the clearances and permits. I—"

"Truly, Captain? Where? Produce them and the charges against you may be reduced some small but measurable fraction."

Lando looked down, seeing his own frame—the thought

whisked by that this might be an unfortunate choice of words—draped in pocketless pajamas much the worse for their recent intimate acquaintance with Teguta Lusat law-enforcement procedures. He looked back up at the governor. "I don't suppose you'd let me go back to my hotel...no, I didn't think so. Well, better yet, check with the Port Authority. They should be able—"

"Captain," the governor sighed with affected weariness, "the Port Authority have no record whatever of any permits being granted to either a Lando Calrissian, or a..." He checked the list again. "...a *Millennium Falcon*. Of this I assure you, sir. In fact, you might say I ascertained the data in the matter *personally*."

"Oh," Lando answered in a small voice, beginning to understand the situation.

"There is also," the governor continued, satisfied now that he had a properly attentive audience, "conspiracy to evade regulations of trade. You see, we know of your attempts to obtain an unlicensed cargo. Carrying a concealed weapon—my, my, Captain, but you *are* a bad boy. Finally: assaulting a duly authorized police officer in an attempt to resist arrest."

The governor got a thoughtful look on his face, looked down at the list again, picked up a stylus and made a note. "*And* failure to settle your hotel bill as you departed those premises.

"*Now* what have you to say?" The governor blinked, licked fat lips in anticipation.

"I see," Lando said, barely concealing his glee. His spirits had begun to lift considerably in spite—or because—of the list of charges against him. The governor was some-one he could deal with, after all.

Ante: "My gun was on the nighttable, it wasn't concealed. And if 'assault' consists of willfully striking a constable in the fist with my stomach, then I'd say you've got me, fair and square. Governor. Sir."

Raise: "Very well, Captain. Or ought I to make that

'*Mister* Calrissian'—you will not likely be doing very much more captaining from now on. What have you to say to the probability of finishing your days doing stoop-labor in the life-orchards amidst other criminals, malcontents, and morons like yourself?"

Lando saw that and raised with a grin: "In all truth, sir, I wouldn't like that very much. I've heard that the life-orchards tend to take it out of you."

The governor nodded, not exactly an easy feat for someone without a discernible neck: "If you had it to begin with, Captain—if you had it to begin with."

Call: "I'd also say you're about to offer me some less-unpleasant alternative. That is, unless you make a custom of trumping up silly charges against every independent skipper who makes your port. And I guess I'd have heard about that long before I got here."

The governor resembled a frowning tree-stump covered in feathers. "Don't anticipate me, Captain, it takes all the fun out of occasions such as this."

He blinked, then pressed a button on his desk.

Lando replaced the cup on its saucer, leaned back in the large soft chair a servant had been ordered to bring him, and drew deeply on one of the governor's imported cigars. Yes, indeed, all of life was one big *sabacc* game, and he was coming out ahead, just as he had done the night before.

The servant—one of the Rafa System's "natives"—offered to pour more tea. *That* had come as a surprise (the native, not the tea). It stood there with a look of worshipful expectancy on its seamed, vacant, elderly gray-hued face. Lando shook his head. One more cup and they could *float* him out of there.

Antoher puff: "You were saying, my dear governor?"

"I was saying, my boy—by the way, are you finding that dressing gown adequate? Your baggage should be here from the hotel by now. But I'd rather we didn't interrupt ourselves at this point in the conversation. I was saying that, among the intelligent species of the galaxy, we humans are a most prolific, preternaturally protean people."

"And alliterative as all get-out, too, apparently." Lando flicked two centimeters of fine gray ash into the vacuum tray on the governor's desk.

Mer ignored the jibe, indicated the stooped and withered servant as it quietly shambled through the main office door behind Lando. "Consider, for example, the Toka—known locally as 'the Broken People.' Entirely devoid of intellect, passion, or will. Subhumanoid in intelligence. Every one of them bears what would be the signs of advanced age among our own kind—white hair, sallow, wrinkled faces, a bent, discouraged gait. Yet these are but superficialities of appearance—or are they?—they carry each of these dubious attributes from birth.

"Domestic animals, really, nothing more. Useful as household servants, they're too unintelligent to be anything but discreet. And in harvesting the life-orchards. But nothing else."

Lando stirred uncomfortably in his chair, adjusting the front of his borrowed bathrobe to conceal his discomfiture. The fabric was velvoid, a revolting shade of purple, sporting bright green-and-yellow trim. If everyone took to using the fabric—and with such egregious taste—he'd have to reassess his entire wardrobe. He wondered precisely what all the palaver was leading up to. He'd heard slavery justified a thousand different ways in a thousand different systems, yet it did seem to him that the Toka lacked some spark, some hint of the aggressive intelligence that made people *people*.

"You said 'for example': 'Consider the Toka for example'—don't you mean 'by contrast'?"

The governor signaled for yet another cup of tea. "Not at all, my dear boy, not at all. With offworld prisoners as overseers, a few droids for technical tasks, the Toka are content to eat food intended for animals, and will quite willingly work themselves to death if it's demanded of them."

Lando allowed himself a small, cynical snort. He'd heard that working in the orchards had some kind of *drainage* effect. Most human prisoners had purely supervisory positions, as the governor had suggested. Ditto for nonhuman sapients that had gotten themselves into trouble. Those unfortunate few "special" prisoners of both classifications, condemned to menial labor, wound up sub-idiots within a year or two. Apparently it didn't affect the Toka that way.

They were already sub-idiots.

"All that must be highly convenient," he said, "for the owners of the orchards."

Mer looked at Lando closely. "The government owns the orchards, my boy, I thought you understood that. The point is, the Toka are quite as human as ourselves."

Lando's jaw dropped. He scrutinized the servant as it poured the governor's tea, oblivious to the highly insulting things being said about it. How could this acquiescent, wizened, hunched, gray-faced nonentity, with its tattered homespun loincloth and thinning white hair, be human?

The governor blinked, managing to look smugly proprietary in spite of it. He opened his mouth to speak...

WHAAAM!

The air was split by an explosion that rocked the office. There was a blinding flash; a column of blue-black smoke boiled into existence, floor-to-ceiling, at the right of the governor's desk.

Oh, brother, Lando thought, *what now?*

FOUR

"*Enough of this!*" The blue-black smoke column shrieked, evaporating into tiny orange sparks that winked and disappeared.

A Sorcerer of Tund, Lando groaned inwardly, how quaint. Members of an allegedly ancient and rather boringly mysterious order from the remote Tund System, they were *all* given to flashy entrances. The rest of the column condensed into a vaguely humanoid figure about Lando's height and general build. The old boy had probably tossed his flashbomb into the office, then stepped through the door quite casually into the center of the smoke.

Nobody was quite sure what species the Tund wizards were, or even if they were all members of the same species. Swathed entirely in the deep gray of his order, the newcomer wore heavy robes that brushed the carpet, totally concealing the form beneath. A turbanlike headdress ended in bands of opaque cloth across the face.

Only the eyes were visible. To his surprise, Lando found

himself wishing fervently that they were not. Despite the absurdity of the sorcerer's melodramatic actions, the eyes told a different, more sobering story: twin whirling pools of—what? Insane hunger of some sort, the gambler decided with a shiver. Those ravenous depths regarded him for a moment as if he were an insect about to be crushed, then turned their malevolent power on the governor, Duttes Mer, who blinked and blinked, and blinked.

"You prolong these preliminaries unnecessarily!" a chilling voice hissed through the charcoal-colored wrappings. Lando couldn't quite determine whether it was a natural utterance or one produced by a vocal synthesizer. "Tell the creature what it needs to know in order to serve us, then dismiss it!"

The governor's composure disintegrated completely. He swiveled his enormous bulk in his chair, short stubby arms half-lifted in unconscious and futile defense, his large yellow eyes rolling with abject terror. His walnut-shaded skin had paled to the color of maple. Even his feathery hair seemed to stir and writhe.

"B-but, Your Puissance, I—"

"Tell the tale, you idiot," the sorcerer demanded, "and be done!"

Lando spat out a bit of ceiling plaster jolted loose by the intruder's showy appearance.

With a terrible effort, the frightened governor turned partially toward Lando, never quite daring to take his eyes altogether off the sorcerer.

"C-captain Land-do Calrissian, p-permit me t-to introduce Rokur Gepta, my...my..."

"*Colleague*," the sorcerer supplied with an impatient hiss that sent goosebumps up the starship captain's spine. It didn't seem to do the governor much good, either. He nodded vaguely, opened his mouth, then slumped in his chair, unable, apparently, to utter another word.

"I see," the sorcerer hissed, taking a step forward, "that *I* shall have to finish this."

Another step forward. Lando fought the urge to retreat through the back of his own chair. "Captain Calrissian, our friend the governor, in his slow, bumbling way, has informed you of the failings of the Toka. They are manifold, I shall warrant, and conspicuous. What this oaf has *not* seen fit to mention thus far—and the very heart and soul of the matter before us—is their most interesting and singularly redeeming feature.

"For you see, despite their humble estate, they observe and practice an ancient system of beliefs which, if taken literally not only explains the present unenviable condition of the Toka, but promises more for the properly prepared and sufficiently daring.

"Much, much more."

The inhuman voice died with a hiss, as if its owner expected some question or remark from the gambler seated before him. Instead, Lando simply looked at the odd figure, forcing himself, despite an inner cringing, to gaze calmly into the lunatic eyes of the sorcerer.

Meanwhile, the governor had managed to recover enough to press a button on his desk, order the Toka servant it summoned to obtain another chair for his "colleague." But the elderly creature could not be induced by kind words (of which the governor uttered but few) of threats (of which he had many in supply) to come near the threatening gray-swathed figure.

In the end, after an embarrassing impasse, Mer himself was forced to rise from his oversized office swiveler, bring the chair in from the next room, and place it for the robed magician. To Lando's amusement, the fat executive had nearly as much difficulty as the Toka forcing himself to come near Rokur Gepta.

Lando himself attempted to relax, settled back, and regarded his cigar, which had long since expired from inattention. Again, seemingly from nowhere, the Toka servant materialized to light it, then, still cowering under the baleful gaze of the sorcerer, vanished once again with a shuffle of bare feet on plush carpet.

"Promises precisely *what?*" Lando asked after a long time, somehow managing to sound casual. Half a hundred wild speculations formed in his mind as he said it, but he repressed them savagely, waiting Gepta out.

"Among other things," the sorcerer whispered, "the Ultimate Instrument of Music."

Great, thought Lando, his fantasies collapsing. It could have been diamonds, platinum, or flamegems; it could have been immortality or Absolute Power; it could have been a good five-microcredit cigar. The guy wants zithers and trombones.

"The Mindharp of Sharu"—Gepta explained as he seated himself, "has been an article of the simple faith among the Toka for centuries uncounted.

"As you are no doubt aware, the current human population of the Rafa—not to mention numerous representatives of many other associated species—dates from the early days of the late, unlamented Republic. What is not generally appreciated by historians is that, in the chaotic, erratically recorded era preceding, a respectable amount of exploration and settlement was also carried out, albeit haphazardly. Thus, when Republican colonists arrived in the Rafa for the first time, they discovered it already occupied by human life.

"The Toka.

"I must explain that, for some decades, I have employed others—anthropologists, ethnologists, and the like, many of them incarcerees of the penal colony here and thus anxious to reduce the burden of their sentences—to observe, record, and analyze the ritual behavior of the Toka, believing that, in the long run, such an effort might produce some particle of interest or profit. I have made many such investments of time and wealth throughout civilized space.

"The Toka, savages that they be, have little or nothing in the way of social organization. Infrequently, however, and at unpredictable intervals, they gather together in small bands for the purpose of ritual chanting, to all appearances the passing-on of a purely verbal heritage.

"Their legends acknowledge that they came, originally, from elsewhere in the galaxy—would-be pioneers and explorers, employing a technology which they subsequently somehow discarded or lost. They, too, found the Rafa already occupied. Their tradition speaks of the Sharu, a super-humanoid race perhaps billions of years advanced in evolution, too terrible to look upon directly or contemplate at any length.

"The Sharu were, of course, responsible for the monumental construction which characterizes this system, a style of architecture betraying a bent of mind so alien that, for the most part, even the purpose of the structures cannot be guessed. It is unclear whether mere contact with the Sharu 'broke' the Broken People, or whether it was the Sharu's later hasty departure.

"For depart they did.

"Legends maintain that their flight was in the face of something even more terrible than they, something they feared greatly, although whether another species, some disease, or some unimaginable something else, we cannot so much as conjecture. They left their massive buildings, they left, apparently, the life-orchards whose original function is as obscure as everything else regarding the Sharu, and they left the Toka, crushed and enfeebled by some aspect of their experience with the Sharu."

Lando reflected on Gepta's words while he let himself be offered another cigar.

It seemed to him that the question of what broke the Broken People was of considerably less pragmatic interest than whatever put such a scare into their superhuman masters. He hated to think of something like that still hanging around the galaxy. A starship captain's life (he knew better from vicarious experience than from any of his own) carried him through many a long, lonely parsec in the darkness. And many a ship has disappeared without so much as a trail of neutrinos to mark its passing.

The Toka servant, skirting Gepta, lit Lando's cigar.

The latter said, finally, "What's all this got to do with me?"

From within the voluminous folds of his ash-colored robes, Gepta extracted an object about the size of a human hand, constructed of some lightweight, bright untarnished golden metal.

It was Lando's turn to blink.

Viewed from one perspective, the device seemed to be a large, three-tined fork—until the gambler looked again. Two tines or four? Or maybe three again? The thing just wouldn't settle down in his field of vision, giving him, instead, the beginnings of a headache when he stared at it too closely or for more than a few seconds.

Gepta placed the object carefully on Duttes Mer's crystalline desk, where it seemed to writhe and pulse without actually moving. The governor gazed down at it with an uninterpretable expression on his face—somewhere between dismay and greed.

"We have reason to believe," Rokur Gepta hissed, "that this object is a Key—perhaps it is a miniature of the Mindharp itself, although that is only surmise. It was ... shall we say, *obtained* in an altogether different system, from a small, shabby museum. But it came originally from the Rafa System and is a Sharu artifact. Of that there is not the slightest doubt."

Somehow, without being told, Lando knew that there were volumes of adventure, betrayal, and deceit behind the sketchy explanation Gepta had just given. He had no doubt it was a story best left untold.

"A key," he repeated. "What the blazes does it unlock, if one may ask?"

"One may ask," the sorcerer replied in a threatening whisper, "but with a great deal more deference and respect in the future than is your customary practice!"

"A thousand pardons!" Lando tried to keep the sarcasm he felt out of his voice, with only partial success. "Pray what does it unlock, noble magician?"

Gepta paused as if trying to gauge Lando's sincerity, then shrugged it off as of no practical consequence. "There is evidence to indicate it provides access to the Mindharp of Sharu. The Mindharp is the focus of a thousand Toka rituals. The fools believe it produced music so sweetly compelling—isn't that just precious!—that it was capable of swaying the most unfeeling of hearts, even across vast distances of space."

The Rafa *was* a multiplanet system, but, given the millions of miles of hard vacuum between planets, Lando reserved judgment. He'd seen legends come to nothing before.

Gepta mentioned that some versions of the legends had the Mindharp as the principal means of communication between the mighty Sharu and their human "pets." What the Mindharp looked like and precisely where it might be found, these questions remained unanswered.

It was up to Lando to answer them.

Or else.

For his part, Lando wondered what the value of such an instrument might be to a system governor or a Sorcerer of Tund. And he wondered again about the terrible unnamed agency which had caused the presumably powerful Sharu to flee their home system like so many panicky mice.

"Okay," he answered finally, "what's in it for me if I find the Mindharp for you?"

The sorcerer turned slightly in his chair, gave Lando the full benefit of his terrifying gaze. "How about your continued liberty?"

For the first time since fetching the sorcerer a chair, Duttes Mer found the wherewithal to speak for himself. "There is also your ship to consider."

"And your life!" Gepta finished in a tone that made Lando's tailbone quiver uneasily.

He ignored it, pretending a nonchalance he didn't feel: "Well," he said, "two out of three isn't bad. I was planning to sell the ship. It's of no use to—"

"That you shall not do, foolish mortal!" Gepta seemed suddenly to swell in size and power. "This entire system is covered with Sharu ruins. We have no idea, as yet, in which of them the Mindharp lies awaiting us. You may very well need the vessel to—"

"Okay, okay. I get your point." Secretly, Lando congratulated himself on having been able to interrupt the sorcerer. He hated being intimidated by anyone and made a practice of *dis*intimidating himself as quickly as he could. "I get a ship I don't want, my life and liberty—which I already had before I stumbled into this rustic metropolis of yours. I don't want to appear unappreciative of your boundless generosity, my dear fellow-beings, but let's negotiate a bonus. A little something for the overhead?"

Mer leaned forward over his desk, not a particularly easy feat considering his treelike torso and the neck nature had seen fit not to endow him with. A threatening look darkened his face as he opened his mouth to speak, but he was stopped short by a hiss from Gepta.

"Incentives, my dear governor, incentives. Do not seal down the intakes of the droids who refine the fuel. We shall indeed offer our brave captain a little something as recompense. Captain Calrissian, would a full cargo of life-crystals from the orchards be acceptable?"

The sorcerer's tone implied it had damn well better be. Mer looked sharply at Gepta. He might be afraid of the gray-robed figure, but it was his bread and butter they were negotiating away. He opened his mouth again, saw that Gepta was serious, and closed it to stifle a groan.

Lando grinned. "I imagine that it will take rather a deal of fancy paperwork to cover up the shortage."

"Which is precisely, my dear Captain"—the sorcerer

turned contemptuously toward Mer, and the governor shrank from his gaze—"what bureaucrats are for."

"Okay, Gepta, so far, so good. But what's to keep you two from seizing my ship and returning me to the tender mercies of the constabulary once I get the Mindharp for you? The most extravagant offer in the universe is a cheap price to pay if you don't intend—"

"Peace!" A long pause for consideration, then: "We shall deliver the cargo to your possession before you begin your search for the Mindharp—*silence, Governor*! However, we shall also have our menials at the port of Teguta Lusat render your *Millennium Falcon* incapable of leaving the system—in case you decide to play us falsely yourself—while leaving it perfectly suitable for travel from planet to planet *within* the system. Once you have secured that which we all seek so ardently, your vessel will be repaired and you will be free to go. Is this agreeable?"

Lando thought. It still wasn't much of a guarantee. In fact, it was the same lousy deal as before, with his ship—or at least its ultralight capacities—as bait instead of the life-crystals. Still, it was all, he was sure, they were going to offer him.

It was a great deal more than he'd expected after Mer's thugs had worked him over.

"All right," he said through a weary sigh that was at least half genuine. "It beats sitting around in jail."

Or having one's mind sucked away by the life-orchards, he thought grimly to himself.

FIVE

"*I* HAVEN'T THE FOGGIEST NOTION! ANYWAY, WHAT POS-
sible business is it of yours?"

Lando stalked moodily along the narrow streetside toward a transit stop. His gaudy shipsuit had at last been
restored to him, even his diminutive stingbeam. This last
decorative touch, he reasoned bitterly, was yet another educational message from Rokur Gepta and Duttes Mer, un-
derlining ironically what they imagined was his utter
helplessness. Well, they'd learn better.

Trouble was, Lando couldn't think of how to accomplish
that at the moment.

Vuffi Raa clattered beside him, carrying the rest of his
luggage, which had been somewhat battered during the assault on the hotel room.

"But Master, I mean, Captain—"

"Call me Lando!"

"Er, Lando, how am I to help you if you won't tell me

what's required of us? I know nothing about what's going on. I spent the entire night in the Confiscated Properties Room at Constabulary headquarters, sandwiched between bales of illicit smoking vegetables and wire baskets overflowing with vibroknives, murder hatchets, and the like."

At the thought, the little droid suffered an involuntary mechanical shudder, which originated at its torso seams and rippled along all five tentacles to their slim-fingered extremities.

Lando's bags bobbed up and down until the seizure passed.

"Did you know," the robot offered in a subdued, conciliatory voice, "that most of the spouse killings in this system are accomplished with cast-titanium skillets?"

Lando stopped suddenly, stared back at Vuffi Raa in anger. "With a sharp blow to the cranium, or simply bad cooking? Look, my mechanical albatross, there's nothing personal in this. It's simply that I haven't the faintest clue where or how to begin the idiot quest they've blackmailed me into, and I stand a far better chance if I *don't* have to spend my time stumbling over a useless—"

"Master, I do not wish to oppose your will in this matter. In fact, such would violate my most fundamental programming to the point of incapacitating me. However—"

"I don't give a damn *what* happens to your capacitors!"

"—however, before you sell me again, I am determined to prove to you that I am, indeed, far from useless. Perhaps even slightly indispensable."

Lando stopped again in the middle of the boardwalk, looking down with contempt at the little suitcase-laden automaton. He took a deep breath.

"*That*, my esteemed collection of clockwork cowardice, would be something to see. What precisely have you in mind?"

Vuffi Raa paused. A lengthy silence followed, and hovercars and repulsor vehicles were suddenly audible swishing by in the narrow, twisted avenue.

Without warning the droid suddenly spoke once more.

"So that is the difficulty; I believe I understand at last. The hotel room. The Constabulary. Your cries to me for help. Your preference, as I understand it, is that I should have been somewhat more, er ... physically demonstrative. Even, perhaps, at the risk of worsening the charges against you?"

Lando turned on a booted heel, wordlessly resumed his march down the street. A bus went by, bearing half a dozen gawking tourists being lectured by the driverdroid on what little was known of the Sharu.

"*Master!*" the droid cried behind him, scurrying to catch up. "There was nothing I could do! I am specifically enjoined by my programming never to—"

"*Stow it!*" Lando snorted, taking some visceral satisfaction in the terse, blue-collar monosyllables. He'd kept his back to Vuffi Raa this time, hadn't even slackened his pace. The robot, with a sudden burst of speed made awkward by his master's bags, slipped around Lando and stopped, blocking the young gambler's further bad-tempered progress.

"Sir, I am not programmed for violence. I cannot harm a sentient being, organic or mechanical, any more than you could flap your arms and fly from this planet."

"Which only goes to show," Lando asserted, startled at the droid's sudden insistent solemnity, "that I was right in the first place." He stepped around the robot and started walking again. "You're useless."

"You are saying, then," the robot's voice inquired, very small, at the captain's rapidly receding back, "that violence is the only solution to this problem, the only capability that is useful or desirable to you in a friend or companion?"

Lando froze, one foot still in the air, stopped dead by the icy disgust he heard in Vuffi Raa's voice. He set the foot down, turned slowly to face the machine. Not only was he arguing with an artifact—he was losing!

Of course the little droid was right. Why else did he,

Lando himself, insist on carrying nothing more than the minimal and miniscule weapon tucked away in his sash? Men of whatever species or construction acted with their minds, survived by their wits. Only a stupid brute would automatically limit himself to the resource of his fists or those of a friend.

That stopped Lando a second time: just exactly when had he begun to consider Vuffi Raa his friend?

"Well, Master," Vuffi Raa mused, "as I understand the situation, you're to search for whatever lock the Key may fit. Yet you haven't any idea whether the lock—and it may be a more metaphorical than material entity—is even on this planet. Correct?"

Lando nodded resignedly. He'd let three regular hover-buses to the spaceport whistle past the stop while he carefully explained things to the droid.

"You've got it, exactly as I just told it to you. So far, old lube-guzzler, you've proved your usefulness as a suit-case caddy and an audio recorder. Any more talents you haven't revealed?"

He shifted on the transit-stop bench so that his back was to the little robot. He wasn't so much annoyed with Vuffi Raa for being useless, as for the fact that the automaton had forced him to confront some of his own failings.

"I beg your pardon, Master, all of my internally lubricated subassemblies are permanently sealed and require no further—"

Lando turned back suddenly. "All right, cut out that robotic literalness. You're a smarter machine than that, and we both know it. What I mean is, do *you* have any ideas? I'm fresh out, myself."

Something resembling a humorous twinkle lived in Vuffi Raa's single red optic for a fleeting moment. "Yes, Master, I have. If I had something ancient and historic, and valuable to look for, I know precisely where I'd look for information. I'd—"

Lando frowned, brightened, and leaped up off the bench. "By the Eternal, of course! Why didn't you say so before? Why didn't *I* think of it? It's certainly worth a try! You may have some use, after all." Lando paced hurriedly down the block just a few yards, turned into the nearest bar, then poked a head back out through the swinging doors.

"Wait for me out here!" he shouted, pointing to a sign in the window of the drinking establishment:

NO SHOES, NO SHIRT, NO EXTEE HELMET FILTERS
NO SERVICE
NO DROIDS ALLOWED

"But Master!" the little robot protested to the empty swinging doors, "I was referring to the public library!"

Having shaken his unwelcomely helpful companion, Lando gratefully entered the cool quiet of the Poly Pyramid, one of Teguta Lusat's many inebriation emporia. There was nothing special about the place appearancewise or otherwise; he'd merely availed himself of the first, nearest ethanol joint on the boardwalk.

He sat down at a table.

What he'd really needed all along, he'd known the minute he left the governor's office, was some kind of Toka gathering of the clans. Unfortunately, life rarely provides what one really needs. To judge from what Gepta had told him, the only people who truly knew what was what where the Sharu were concerned were much too primitive to *hold* conventions—or much of anything else. They had no villages, no tribes, not even any real nuclear families.

Every now and again, at unpredictable intervals, the Toka simply collected in small bunches to bay at the moon like wild canines. Rafa IV didn't *have* a moon, but, Lando thought, it was the principle that counted.

All right, the young gambler reasoned, one place he'd noticed the reliable presence of Toka—even before he'd known who and what they were—was in saloons, usually swamping the floors and polishing spitoons, the kind of occupation reserved in other systems for lower-classification droids. Here, the innkeepers could afford to entertain their prejudices and those of their clientele against the mechanical minority; Toka semislaves were handier and far cheaper.

Lando looked around. He'd selected a table in the approximate center of the room, halfway toward the back, and halfway between the bar that ran down the left side of the place, and the booth-lined wall opposite. Ordinarily, he'd prefer a position where he could see everything that went on and not have to turn his back to the door, perhaps something toward the rear.

Now the important thing was to *be* seen.

The Poly Pyramid was a working-being's establishment. On the walls, lurid paintings alternated with sporting scenes from a dozen systems. On a less cosmopolitan planet, racy shots of unclad females would predominate, but, in places where one being's nude was another's nightmare, sensuality had given way before such items as incompetently taxidermized galactic fauna, which were nailed to the walls or suspended on wires from the ceiling: fur-bearing trout from Paulking XIV, for example, and a jackelope from Douglas III.

As bars go, it was brightly lit and noisy, especially considering the small number of patrons so early in the afternoon. On both sides of the traditional louvered doors the inner, full-length doors were propped open with a pair of giant laser drill-bits, souvenirs of the deep-bore mining of Rafa III, whose vacationing practitioners habituated the place.

In the back, the ubiquitous native was emptying ashtrays over a waste can.

The bartender, a scrawny specimen of indeterminate middle age, approached Lando, wringing his knobbly hands in a dark green apron. What little hair he still possessed was restricted to the back and sides of his otherwise highly reflective pate, and cut short. He had a nose friends might have called substantial, others spectacular. Tattooed permanently beneath it, a mild sneer, punctuated by a small mole on his chin.

"Spacers' bars're all downtown about three blocks, Mac," he said in a peculiar drawl. "This here's a hardrock miners' joint."

Lando raised an eyebrow.

"Ain't sayin' y'can't drink here. Just likely y'won't want to—once the off-shift R and R crew starts t'fillin' the place up."

It seemed a long speech for the wiry little man. He stood there, balanced on the balls of his feet, relaxed but ready, looking down at Lando from under half-closed eyelids, a foul-smelling cigar butt dangling from his mouth. A large, dangerous-looking lumpiness was apparent beneath one side of his apron bib.

Lando nodded slightly. "Thanks for the advice; I'm meeting somebody here. Have you a pot of coffeine to hand?" Until he'd sat down, he'd almost forgotten the night's sleep he'd lost. Now it was catching up to him.

"Some of m'best friends drink it," the barkeep replied. "One mug comin' up."

He began to walk away, then paused and turned back to Lando. "Remember what I said, Mac. Splints an' bandages'll cost ya extra."

Lando nodded again, extracted one of the governor's cigars from a breast pocket, and settled back. Then, casually, he pulled the Key from an inside pocket. An optometrist's nightmare, it wouldn't hold still visually, even locked firmly in his hands. First it seemed to have three branches, then two, depending on your viewpoint. If you didn't shift the angle you were watching it from, it would oblige by shifting it for you. Lando averted his eyes.

He sat like that for forty-five minutes without any seeming reaction from anyone. Having long since finished his coffeine and tired of the cigar, at last he rose, left a small tip on the table, nodded amiably at the gnarled little bartender, and stepped outside onto the boardwalk.

"Master?"

"Don't call me Master! Let's find another bar."

SIX

THE NEXT PLACE SPORTED A SMALL BRONZE PLAQUE BE-side the door that stated: "FACILITIES ARE NOT PROVIDED FOR MECHANOSAPIENTS."

It meant "No droids allowed."

And it wasn't even true, not in its original rendering. Vuffi Raa had a sort of waiting room to park himself in, nicely furnished, quiet, with recharging receptacles. Only bigotry of the very nicest, highest-class sort was practiced there. Lando left the robot with a couple others of its kind watching a domestic stereo serial.

Inside, three Toka swampers were distributing dirty water evenly all over the floor. That they and their employers probably thought they were washing only demonstrated that pretensions and sanitation don't necessarily go together.

It was not quite dark, so the real drinking crowd hadn't arrived there yet, either. It didn't matter; Lando wasn't interested in them.

Nearly an hour went by this time, Lando sipping a hot stimulant and toying discreetly with the Key. The thing was as evasive to the tactile senses as it was visually, he discovered, closing his eyes and examining it by touch. "Perverse" might be a better word, and even more nauseating, somehow. He opened his eyes with something resembling relief.

On several occasions, he could have sworn that one or another of the natives was staring at him intently when he wasn't looking in their direction.

Which was also precisely what he'd expected. He began to allow himself a feeble hope.

Another hour, and two more saloons, brought him back to the Spaceman's Rest, the first such establishment he'd visited in Teguta Lusat, the day before. It seemed like a thousand years ago. The double-moustached alien proprietor was nowhere to be seen so early in the evening, but the droid behind the bar seemed to have had his memory banks attended to. He recognized Lando with a cordial mechanical nod.

By then, the gambler was thoroughly coffeed out. He leaned against the bar, ordered a real drink, then took it back to a table and sat, unobtrusively displaying the weird, eye-straining Key as before, for everyone to see.

One thing *was* different about the place: its multispecies clientele and robot bartender encouraged Lando not to leave Vuffi Raa outside in the street. After all, the little fellow was an item of valuable property (to somebody, someday, Lando hoped), and probably wouldn't like being stolen, either.

That small mechanical worthy presently bellied—figuratively speaking—up to the bar, cutting up electronic touches while the 'tender polished glasses. Lando had always wondered what robots talked about among themselves, but never enough to eavesdrop.

Despite the tolerant atmosphere of the Spaceman's Rest,

the usual Toka flunky was there, an elderly wretch distributing synthetic plastic sawdust on the floor from a bucket. Lando grew hopeful as the shavings around his table deepened to two or three times the thickness of those covering the rest of the barroom floor.

The Toka kept circling, reluctant yet fascinated, rather like an insect around a bright light. He stared at the Key, tossed a worried glance toward the bar, then turned back to the Key again, drawn irresistibly. If he was concerned about the bartender's reaction, he needn't have bothered; the droid didn't even seem to notice, wrapped up as he was in his work and in conversation with Vuffi Raa. Maybe native productivity wasn't his department.

On an odd impulse to see what would happen, Lando tucked the Key back into his pocket.

Abruptly, the Toka dropped his pail with a crash and bolted out through the back of the room, leaving a fabric door-drape swinging behind him and a few gaping mouths among the sparse scattering of customers. Ordinarily nothing would induce the lethargic and prematurely senile natives to do *anything* in a hurry.

Lando held his breath: could his lucky break have come so soon?

He signaled the 'tender for another drink. Vuffi Raa obliged by bringing it over to the gambler.

"I still think we'd make better progress in the library, Master." He set the glass on the dark polished wood of the tabletop. Lando was having a *talmog* that evening, one part spiced ethanol to one part Lyme's rose juice, popular in a unique sunless, centerless system many hundreds of light-years away. It burned. Lando hated the things, which made them another drink he could nurse and re-ice all night if he had to.

"Listen, little friend, let me do the detecting. For your information, I think I've got a bite already."

"A bite, Master?" The robot reached a free tentacle to

the floor, scooped up a pinch of sawdust, and held it closely to his large red eye. "I would have thought the place to be cleaner kept than that. Perhaps the Board of Sanitation—"

"Vuffi Raa, how would you like to be reprocessed into sardine cans?"

For the second time that afternoon, there was mirth in the robot's eye. *"Master—"*

"Don't call me—" Lando stopped. The sawdust-spreader who had observed the gambler so closely was holding back the hanging for a veritable grandfather-of-grandfathers among the grandfatherly natives—a wizened, shriveled super-ancient nearly doubled over with the burden of his long life.

The bartender had stopped his glass cleaning, stood silent as he watched the geriatric native hobble toward the gambler. The old man's straight white hair hung in matted tangles to his shoulders.

"Lord," the ancient Toka wheezed almost inaudibly, bowing until his forehead touched the tabletop. "It is as it was told. Thou art the Bearer and the Emissary. That which thou concealest is indeed the Fabled Key lost long ago."

The other Toka was suddenly nowhere to be seen. Somehow the spell was broken. The barkeep gave a metal-jointed shrug, resumed his work.

"I, er . . ."

Now that Lando had made his contact, he realized he didn't quite know what to do with it. The ancient glanced at Vuffi Raa. Lando gave the little droid a scowl, which failed to rid him of the machine at what could be a delicate point in the proceedings. Vuffi Raa remained standing by the table, all attention focused on the old Toka.

"Lord," the worthy repeated. "I am Mohs, High Singer of the Toka. Knowest thou what thou holdest on thy person?" The elderly character straightened—as much as he was ever going to again in this life—and Lando noticed a tattoo on his forehead, a crude line drawing of the Key itself.

"An unaccountably odd artifact," he answered, unconsciously patting the irregular lumpiness of it in his inside jacket pocket. "Some kind of three-dimensional practical joke. But, please—sit down. Would you like something to drink?"

The ancient glanced around, a furtive expression tucked deeply into the wrinkles in his face. The tattoo puckered on his forehead.

"Such is not permitted, Lord. I—"

"Master," the droid interrupted again.

"Shut up, Vuffi Raa! Well, old fellow," he said turning to Mohs, "wilt —*will* you at least tell me something more about the Key?" He took it out, held it in his hand.

Mohs had to wheeze a little while before he could get the words out. "Thou wishest to test thy servant, then? So must it be, Lord. Thy wish is my command."

The Toka launched into a long, whining gargle in a language that was vaguely familiar to Lando. Perhaps it was an obscure dialect from some system he'd visited.

The effect on the dozen or so other patrons wasn't exactly salutory: they watched and listened, but Lando couldn't persuade himself to believe the expressions on their faces were friendly. He found himself wishing he'd sat a little nearer the door.

The Toka's monolog went on and on, one of Mohs' bony hands indicating the Key occasionally, the rest of the time his weathered face turned upward toward the ceiling. Finally, the chanting ceased.

"Have I recited rightly, Lord?"

Lando scratched his smoothly shaven chin. "Sure. Perfectly. And—just as another test, mind you—let's have an abbreviated version in the vernacular." He indicated the rest of the room. "Might win a few converts among the heathen. Think you're up to it?"

"Lord?"

The old man reached out shakily toward the Key, apparently thought better of it, withdrew the gnarled hand with obvious reluctance, then began. "This is the Key of the Overpeople, Lord Bearer, the Opener of Mysteries. It is the Illuminator of Darkness, the Shower of the Way. It is the Means to the End. It is—"

"Hold it, Mohs, just tell me what it does."

"Why, Lord, as thou knowest perfectly well..."

Mohs tapered off. Was that a hint of sudden skepticism in the ancient High Singer's eye? He began again, in a very slightly different tone of voice.

"It releaseth the Mindharp of the Sharu, which in turn—"

"Bull's Eye! Look, Mohs. As official Bearer of the Key, I have personally selected you to lead—in a purely ceremonial sense, of course—to lead a pilgrimage. We're going to use the Key. What do you think of that?"

The thought that everything was happening too easily began to seep into the back of Lando's mind, but he repressed it savagely. He was stuck with his task and welcomed any lead that would get it over with.

"Why, whatever else would we do, Lord? It must be as it has been told, else it would not have been told to begin with."

"I'm sure there's a hole in your logic somewhere, but I'm too tired right now to go poking for it. How soon can you start, then?"

The old man raised his snowy eyebrows, and the crude representation of the Key on his forehead squashed itself from top to bottom like an accordion.

"This very instant, Lord, if that be thy desire. Nothing supercedeth Their holy plan."

He cast a pious eye toward the ceiling fixtures again.

"Good," the gambler answered, once the native's gaze returned from its rafter rapture, "but I think we'll—"

"Master!" The little droid's tone was urgent.

"What is it, Vuffi Raa?"

"Master, I hear trouble coming!"

"Just what we needed." Lando groaned.

Suddenly, a man with a gun in his hand burst through the door.

"All right, spaceboy," he growled, pointing his massive weapon at the gambler, "get ready to die!"

SEVEN

"*M*R. *JANDLER!*" THE BARKEEP SHOUTED, A PANICKY harmonic apparent in its electronic voice. "I'm terribly sorry, sir, but my employer has permanently restricted you from entering this—"

"Shut up, machine! Now where in blazes was I? Oh, yeah—you there! Yeah, I'm talkin' to you! It's just like Bernie down to the Pyramid told me! And not only with a snivelin', job-stealin' droid at the table, but a dirty Toka, too! What are you sailor, some kinda pervert?"

The few patrons in the establishment instantly cleared a broad aisle between Lando and the intruder.

"I don't know," Lando replied evenly. "It wasn't my turn to watch. Now just who in the galaxy are *you*?"

The man was good-sized, maybe eighty-five kilos, perhaps a shade under two meters tall. Over the powder-blue jumpsuit that draped his broad frame, he wore a dark blue tunic and neckcloth. He was neat, clean, shaved, and surprisingly sober for a thug, Lando thought. And with surprisingly good taste, as well.

The man walked closer; the muzzle of his pistol didn't waver.

The robot bartender hurried to Lando's table, placing himself between the two men. "He's the former owner of the Spaceman's Rest, Captain Calrissian, that was before I worked here. When the place changed hands, he tried to get a clause put in the agreement, never to allow—"

"What do you mean 'tried,' you miserable junk heap? A contract is a contract! People got a right to make any contract they want!"

Apparently undecided whether to shoot the young gambler or the bartender, Jandler was waving his gun around in a manner that tied knots in Lando's stomach. If it came to a choice, Lando hoped he'd choose the bartender as less messy—the bigot did seem to have some aesthetic sensitivities. The robot stood its ground.

"Not when there's a system-wide ordinance against discrimination, sir, and especially not when you lost the place in a table game to a being who doesn't believe in discrimination."

The man swiveled on the machine—Lando thought about jumping him just then, but it remained a thought—and brought the weapon down hard on its plexisteel dome-top with a sickening crunch!

"That for your ordinance!" he hollered, "and *that—OWCH!*"

"You should never kick a droid, sir," Vuffi Raa advised sympathetically as the man hopped around on one foot, cursing. Somehow Jandler found the concentration to peer menacingly at the starfish-shaped robot.

"Quite right," Lando offered, diverting Jandler's attention even further. "He might have another droid. *Sic 'im, Vuffi Raa!*"

Jandler whirled on Vuffi Raa again. The five-tentacled 'bot stared at his master in bewilderment, but the distraction worked. The stranger took an ugly step toward Vuffi Raa, on his guard against the totally harmless little droid, and the bartender, despite its severely dented cranium, walloped the fellow on the back of the neck with a chair Lando toed over toward it.

Jandler went down like a sack of mynock guano.

A cheer rose from the dozen or so patrons in the room. They began gathering about Lando's table—somewhat unjustly ignoring the injured and heroic 'tender—lining up to shake the gambler's hand and pat him on the back.

"I'm gratified," Lando observed with a highly necessary shout—he hadn't so much as risen from his chair during the excitement and was taking a far worse beating now from his new admirers—"I'm gratified to see that not all robots are programmed categorically against violence." More specifically to the crowd he said, "Thanks, it was nothing, honestly, thank you very much."

"He's only programmed against *starting* it, sir," the bartender answered. "I'll just haul this fellow out in the street now, if you don't mind. By way of restitution for the disturbance, will you have a drink on the house?"

"I'd rather have it on the table in front of me. And bring one for my friend, here. Mohs?"

Lando jumped up. Mohs was gone.

So was the Key.

Turning quickly, Lando glimpsed the raveled tail of a gray-rag garment whisk through the door-drape at the back of the room. He was through the little crowd and across the room with a speed that startled even the robots.

He grabbed—

And received a collection of knobbly knuckles in the teeth!

Spitting blood, Lando seized the wrist attached to the knuckles, bit down hard in the meaty edge of the palm. Mohs let out a yelp and brained his erstwhile Lord lefthanded with the Key. Releasing the old man's arm, a dazed, surprised, and angry Lando went for the throat with both hands, catching Mohs' knee, instead, right between the legs.

Lando groaned and sank down to his knees, fighting the urge to vomit.

This, however, put him in a position of advantage. As the elderly native—Lando couldn't make himself stop thinking of the savage in this manner—came in for another shot with the Sharu Key, Lando grabbed the nearest naked, dirty ankle that came to hand. Mohs went down on his back, with Lando on top, the old man biting and scratching.

By this time, Vuffi Raa had made it to his master's side, where he hopped up and down, shouting advice that Lando couldn't hear and probably wouldn't have followed. It was scarcely a fair fight. As much as he would have liked to, Lando couldn't punch the "helpless" old fellow into submission. He simply attempted to hold on and ride the furious storm to its conclusion.

They rolled across the storeroom, crashing into crates and cartons, and at one point fetching up against the lower extremities of the bartender, who had joined Vuffi Raa in supervising and kibitzing. For a brief crystalline moment, Lando looked up.

"You're being a lot of help," he said to the bartender.

The mixerbot remained motionless. "Beating up old men is a little out of my line, Captain. Besides, you look like you could use the practice."

Abruptly, Lando was sucked back into the fight. Mohs bashed him on the head again, but a bit more weakly. Lando grabbed the Key, then managed to lever himself into a sitting position astride the Toka Singer, grab a forelock of shaggy white mane, and bounce the elderly head once, gently but firmly, on the floor.

Mohs struggled for another moment, then relapsed into passivity.

"Naughty, naughty, Mohs," Lando said, gasping for breath as he looked down at the ancient. "No fair doing holy things without the duly constituted Key Bearer's help."

Mohs concealed his face in his long, emaciated hands. "Thou mayest kill me now, Lord. I have sinned greatly."

With considerable effort, Lando cranked himself back into a standing position, reached a hand down to the native, and helped him up.

"By the Emptiness, that's the first sign of spirit I've seen from any of you people."

He sat down, panting, on a stack of plastic cartons in the dingy rear hall. "But, from now on, just keep in mind who's the sacred emissary here, will you?" He held up the Key. "I'm in charge of this eyeball-bender for the duration. Keep that in mind, and we'll get along fine. Vuffi Raa?"

The robot trundled up beside him, his tentacles a tangle of nervous excitement. "Yes, Master? Sorry I couldn't help you back there, but—"

"I know, I know. In your estimation, how long will it take for Gepta's crew to sabotage the *Falcon* the way they said they were going to?"

The droid considered: "Not more than an hour, Master. It's merely a matter of unshipping the toroidal dis—"

"Spare me the technical details." Lando turned to the old man, who seemed to be recovering more quickly than he was. "Mohs, we're headed for the spaceport to begin our little excursion. Are you ready to come along and behave?"

The old man nodded humbly, bowing. "Yes, Lord, I am."

"Then let's get moving—and don't call me Lord."

Mohs stole a glance at Vuffi Raa, nodded again. "Yes, Master."

"Mohs," Lando scrutinized the wrinkled figure carefully, "are you trying to be funny?"

"What is 'funny,' Lord?"

Lando sighed, beginning to be resigned to permanent exasperation. "Something about this whole confounded setup. Here I neatly avoid a messy conflict with that character out in the bar, and then you go and try to set yourself up in the Key Bearer business. And I don't see why Gepta and his pocket-piece governor need me to do their dirty work in the first place. They had the Key, why not just...Come on, Vuffi Raa, we're getting out of here. I need a chance to think. We'll doss down aboard the *Falcon* tonight and get a fresh start in the morning."

He paused, then added, "And I want you to help me rig up a few booby traps in case anybody else wants to try grabbing the Key."

"Master, I'm not sure my programming will allow that!"

The bartender stood, impassive, then turned and went back into the bar. "Good luck, sir. I think you're going to need it."

Keeping a suspicious eye glued to Mohs, Lando said to Vuffi Raa, "Very well, then, whether we can overcome your cybernetic scruples or not, we're *still* spending the night aboard the *Falcon*. Get out front and find us some transport—a bus, a vegetable gravlifter, anything." He shrugged uncomfortably, trying to unwind a painfully twisted muscle in his shoulder. "Do you think they might have any taxis on this misbegotten mudball?"

The robot knew a rhetorical question when he heard one.

Lando watched him go, rubbed at his bruised shoulder, stood up and stretched.

"Stay a moment, Lord." It was the old Toka. "It is not meet that thy servant mount the same conveyance as thyself."

Lando snorted. "What do you propose as an alternative?"

Mohs shook his snowy head. "Worry not, Lord, neither trouble thyself over the minor travails of thy servant, but go thou, instead, thine own way, even as thy servant shall go his."

"Catchily put. Does that mean you'll meet us at the spaceport?"

The old man looked puzzled. "Is that not what I just said?"

"Somewhere in there, I suppose; it got lost in the tran-substantiation. Very well, old disciple, have it your own way." Blast, there was a snag in his tailored uniform trousers. They simply weren't intended for brawling. "We'll leave a light burning in the starboard viewport."

He left by the front door to join Vuffi Raa. Mohs presumably exited through the back. A hoverbus swooshed along almost immediately. Lando and the robot were whisked the ten kilometers to the landing field in as many minutes.

They were not unanticipated.

"What in the name of the Core is that?" Lando asked the equally astonished droid.

Outside the chain-link gate that filled a gap between the force-field pole-pieces around the port, a considerable and highly unusual crowd had gathered. Absently, Lando paid the driver droid, turned to stare at the hundreds of stooped gray figures standing in their loincloths in the moonless dark, chanting to the cold unanswering stars.

As the gambler and his companion approached them, the primitives stepped back *en masse*, forming a broad, open corridor. To one side, a spaceport security officer was visible through the transparency of his guard booth, gesticulating at the visicom.

Lando and Vuffi Raa, the former growing more reluctant by the minute to surround himself in an unpredictable mob—especially after his recent wrestling match with one of the natives—made slow, involuntarily stately progress as the crowd folded itself back before them, the rhythmic chanting never missing a beat.

At the end of the living aisle, they encountered Mohs.

EIGHT

IT HAD BEEN A COUPLE OF VERY LONG SLEEPLESS DAYS. Lando didn't even want to think about how an ancient savage on foot had beaten a fusion-powered hovercraft across ten kilometers of twisted, ruin-strewn thoroughfare to the spaceport.

Let the robot figure it out, he told himself groggily, that's what Class Two droids are for.

Mohs, High Singer of the Toka, had, of course, been leading the high-pitched, disharmonious chant. Now the old man signaled the others to provide a more subdued background music as he addressed the gambler:

"Hail, Lord Key-Bearer"—he turned to Vuffi Raa—"and Emissary. It is, indeed, as it has been told. Long have we awaited thee. Vouchsafe now unto thy servants what it is that shall next come to pass."

"We shall climb aboard yon *Millennium Falcon*," Lando pointed to the crablike vessel sitting on the asphalt a hundred meters away, and yawned. "Tuck ourselves into our little beddy-byes, a get some—*yipe!*"

He stopped short. Across the tarmac, half a dozen repulsor-trucks, overhead lights blazing like novas, surrounded the small starship. Along with what appeared to be at least two squads of heavily armed constabulary.

"Good grief," the gambler said to the robot. "Your ethical virtue will remain unscathed tonight, at least. *Everybody* seems to have beaten us to the spaceport. So much for the wonders of public transportation. What do you suppose we've done now?"

"'We,' Master?"

"Very funny, my loyal and trusty droid. Your support underwhelms me."

Approaching the lowered boarding ramp, Lando, the robot, and the Toka Singer—who had detached himself from his departing congregation—were met by armored, dark-visored cops, blasters drawn and at the ready.

"Okay, officer, I'll pay the two credits." Lando was tired and angry. He didn't even want to know how they'd gotten in past the locking-up he'd done the previous night. But he kept his tone goodnatured. With those fellows, it paid to.

"Good evening, Captain," came an equally good-humored reply from beneath a helmet with two decorative bars across its highly reflective forehead. "We're here to guard your cargo while it's being loaded."

"Really?" Lando marveled. He was always suspicious of favors from policemen. The trooper pointed an armored finger toward the trucks, from which a steady stream of packages ran up automated conveyors into the *Falcon*'s open cargo hatches.

"That's right," the guardsman answered, then added in a more subdued and, Lando thought, somehow civilian tone, "I sure hope your bruises are healing up okay. We were pretty careful. Nothing personal, you understand, sir. A guy has orders to follow."

And plenty of morally evasive clichés to fall back on, Lando thought as he peered into the anonymous helmet visor. He gave it up. "Think nothing of it, my dear fellow, I understand completely. I'll try and do as much for you, someday."

The cop chuckled, snapped to attention, clicked booted heels, and brought his heavy handweapon to port arms. Lando suppressed an unmilitary snigger of his own at the display, and climbed aboard the *Falcon* with Vuffi Raa and Mohs behind him.

The interior of the *Millennium Falcon*, Lando thought for the hundredth time, was more like the innards of some great living beast than the inanimate human construction that it was. Starliners and other vessels he was familiar with were as rectilinear and orderly as the hotel where he'd spent an uncomfortable night in Teguta Lusat. But aboard his ship were no separate compartmentalized cabins of any sort, nor any clear demarcation between cargo and living space, simply lots of unspecialized volume, currently being rapidly and compactly filled with cartons and crates of highly valuable life-crystals.

Lando watched the port's longshorebots work. It appeared Gepta was more than keeping his part of the bargain—Lando made a note to have the crystals assayed as soon as possible. There was nothing about the sorcerer, or his governmental flunky, that inspired trust, even had Lando been the trusting type.

Parking Mohs at a convenient bulkhead frame, Lando and Vuffi Raa stopped off beside the ultralightspeed section of the ship's drive area. There had been some changes made. And not for the better, Lando thought.

"Oh, Master!" the dismayed Class Two robot wailed. "Just see what they have done to her!" He rushed to the faster-than-light drive panels and stood, wringing his metallic tentacles and making the kind of high-pitched squeal humans call tinnitis and see physicians about.

All along the wall, access panels had been left rudely hanging open. Frayed wires and broken cables dangled from the overhead. Small bits and pieces of machinery, mechanical detritus such as nuts and washers and scraps of insulation littered the decking. The faint foul stench of soldering and scorched plastic defied the ventilating system's best efforts.

"It's quite a mess, all right, old home appliance. But don't fret, she's only a machine, after all, and they've promised to make full and complete repairs, once we—"

"Only a machine?" The robot's voice was disbelieving, scandalized, and almost hysterical. "Master, I, too, am 'only a machine'! This is horrible, unbearable, cruel, evil. It's—"

"Oh, come now, Vuffi Raa, don't exhaust your vocabulary. You're a *sentient* machine. The *Falcon's* big and smart, but she's way, way beneath you on the scale of things. Otherwise I shouldn't have had to rent that confounded, idiotic—"

"Master," the droid interrupted, more gently this time, "how does it make you feel to see somebody's furry pet run over by the roadside? Do you dismiss it, say it's only an animal, beneath you on the scale of things? Or do you feel like . . . well, the way I feel now?"

Lando shook his head, too tired to argue further. The point, within limits, was certainly well taken. And he hated to think that the little automaton was a more humane being than he himself.

"I'm going forward," he said abruptly. "There's no telling what trouble somebody like Mohs can find to get into with all those dials and pretty buttons going unsupervised."

"Very well, Master. With your permission, I'll remain here a little while to comfort her as best I can and tidy up this . . . this butchery."

"As you will." Lando paused in the bight of curving corridor, turned back to see the droid collecting washers and sheared rivets from the decking. "Er, uh, sorry I didn't understand your feeling at first, old cybernet. It's just that I..." His voice trickled off.

There was a long silence between the two, then: "That's all right, Lando. At least you understood after I explained it. That's more than most organic beings could do, I think."

The gambler cleared his throat self-consciously. "Yes, well, er, ah... see you forward in a little while, then—and don't call me Lando."

In the tubular cockpit forward, Lando took an inexpert look at the indicator lights on various control boards, then thumbed through the *Falcon*'s dog-eared flight manual to see what they meant.

Mostly, the unfamiliar lights he saw were warnings of open hatch covers where the loading was being carried out. Clunks and thumps and groans below confirmed the telltales. The entire section of instrumentation given over to the ultralight drive had only solid reds and yellows glaring balefully.

Behind Lando, in the high-backed jumpseat where the gambler had placed him firmly, Mohs seemed to have lapsed back into senile passivity. Lando couldn't blame him: he almost wished he could do the same. It had been a long, hard day for the poor old savage. The Toka sat, eyes wide open, staring down at the decking plates, knobbed hands lying palms up in loinclothed lap.

"Mohs?" Lando asked gently.

The old man started, as if he'd been thoroughly asleep despite the open eyes and hadn't seen Lando turn around to speak to him. He blinked, rubbed a slow and shaky hand over his stubbly chin.

"Yes, Lord?"

"Mohs, what was it you and your people were chanting out there by the fence?"

The old man breathed deeply, resettled himself in the

heavily padded jumpseat. He'd never placed his scrawny fundament in so luxurious a resting place before. He patted the arms a little, almost in disbelief.

"It was the Song of the Emissary, Lord, in honor of the advent of you and—"

"I see."

A long, thoughtful few moments followed. The old man's breathing was almost loud in the control cabin. Lando hadn't really thought very much about this Emissary business. There hadn't been time. It was beginning to dawn on him that there might be more to all the chanting and Key-Bearing stuff than Gepta had seen fit to tell him.

"Well, old fellow," Lando said, not unkindly, "if you're not too played out after all the excitement, why don't you tell me—"

With a clank at the doorsill betraying whatever weary clumsiness robots happen to experience, Vuffi Raa chose that moment to return from the drive area aft, clambered into the right-hand seat, which Lando had replaced after sending the pilot droid back to the Oseon. The little automaton was uncharacteristically subdued.

"Everything shipshape and tidy to your liking, then?" Lando asked conversationally. "Good. Did you happen, by the way, to overhear that guard captain out there? He more or less directly identified himself as the unreconstituted son-of-a—"

"Yes, Master," the robot responded somewhat dully. "I must say, it was something of a surprise."

Lando mused. "I don't know about that. I don't suppose it's all that great a coincidence. In the first place, they can't have an endless supply of uniformed thugs to call upon in Teguta Lusat to do their dirty work. And in the second place, assigning that particular one to greet us would be Duttes Mer's idea of a joke. Actually, I thought it rather sporting of the fellow to apologize and ask after my health and all that sort of thing."

Once more imitating human beings, Vuffi Raa did a

double take, turning to "face" Lando. "And especially considering the effective way in which you got even, afterward, Master."

It was Lando's turn to blink surprise. "Got even? What in the name of the Galactic Drift do you mean?"

"Why, Master, I thought we were talking about the *same* so-called coincidence. Aren't you aware of who that—"

"Certainly: the paramilitary bully from the hotel, last night."

"And more recently, Master, a civilian 'Mr. Jandler' from the Spaceman's Rest. I thought you recognized his voice, as I did—and the painful stiffness with which he moved his neck."

"You don't say!"

Perhaps there is some justice in the universe, after all, Lando thought with satisfaction. Then he screwed his face up sourly: another blasted mystery! What had that charade in the saloon been all about, then? He'd taken it for a bit of bigoted random stupidity on a highly bigoted and randomly stupid planet. And what did it all imply about the robot bartender (or its owner), who seemed—

A previous idea demanded Lando's attention quite suddenly: "Tell us about the Emissary, Mohs, old fellow—no, *don't* sing it! Make it short, intelligible, and to the point."

The Toka ancient stirred. "Legend foretelleth of a dark adventurer, an intrepid star-sailor with preternatural luck at games of chance, who shall come with a weird inhuman companion in silvery armor arrayed. They shall possess the Key with which to liberate the Mindharp, which in turn shall liberate the—"

Lando slammed a palm on the armrest of his chair. "Well, I'll be double-dyed, hornswoggled, and trussed up like a holiday fowl! We were set up, Vuffi Raa! Gepta must have had his convict spies watching the port for months—possibly years—to find a sucker with the right qualifications: gambler, spaceship-captain, with an unenameled droid and a weak mind. That's why neither a creepy old Tund magician nor that ugly neckless governor of his could play this hand themselves: they don't fit the Toka legend!"

"And we do, Master?"

"Ask Mohs, here; he's the local Keeper of the Flame."

"Master?"

"Never mind, a figure of speech. Let's go back aft and get some shut-eye. We've got some heroing to do in the morning—and don't forget to polish your armor, old can-opener!"

NINE

Came the dawn, with a full night's rest under his stylish if somewhat wrinkled satyn semiformal cummer-bund, Lando was in a worse mood than ever. He loathed the idea that he might have been taken by one of the marks, and the nasty suspicion was growing within him that he'd only begun to discover the extent to which he'd been out-maneuvered by Rokur Gepta.

The takeoff of the *Millennium Falcon* shortly after sun-rise, had proceeded as smoothly as clockwork, as fluidly graceful as a textbook exercise. Even the Teguta Lusat con-trol tower had complimented Lando on it. This failed to cheer him. He passed the compliments along to Vuffi Raa, who had been at the controls.

The troopers and freight-handlers had departed sometime the previous evening under the cover of the moonless sky, sealing the *Falcon*'s hatches tightly behind them until the control boards displayed a solid, unbroken tapestry of green pilot lamps. Mohs had curled up on a lounger, snoring like some impossible archaic internal combustion engine. Vuffi Raa had tidied up and tinkered through the night.

Sapient robots do need sleep—the brighter they are the greater the need—but Lando never had been able to discern a pattern in their nightly habits. He himself had tossed and turned, sweating into the fancy and expensive synsilk bed-roll he'd spread under the common-room gaming table, and finally achieving an unrestful semiconsciousness from which the robot had awakened him, stiff and groggy. Several large containers of hot, black coffeine had only deepened his already gruesome mood.

"All right," he snarled unnecessarily at the old Toka shaman. They were forward in the cockpit once again, Mohs perched on the jumpseat, Vuffi Raa occupying the right-hand copilot's couch as a token concession to the human captain, but very much in control of the ship. Someday, thought Lando, when it all was over, he'd sell both blasted machines, Vuffi Raa and the *Millennium Falcon*, to some-one fully capable of appreciating them.

"So where do we go from here?"

They were lying in a close orbit around Rafa IV. From there they could reach any point on the planet's surface within minutes or strike out freely across space for any other body in the system. Mohs closed his eyes, mouthed the rote-memorized words of an ancient ritual to himself, and finally pointed a dessicated finger out the viewport.

"Lord, the Mindharp lieth in that direction."

Perfect, Lando thought sourly to himself, I've got a me-chanical kid's toy for a pilot, and an elderly witch doctor for a navigator! A sadistic little voice inside him insisted on adding that he also had a *sabacc*-playing conman for a captain. Even all around, then. He gave it up and peered through the faceted transparency.

How in the devil do you discuss the details of navigational astronomy with an utter savage? "You mean that bright light in the heavens, there, Mohs?"

"Of a certainty, Lord: the fifth planet of the Rafa System; it possesseth two natural satellites, a breathable atmosphere, and approximately nine-tenths of a standard gravity, not unlike Rafa IV beneath us, whence we came—except in the matter of the moons. Is it not pleasing in thy—"

"Forget it!" The gambler peered suspiciously at the old man. "How is it that you know so blasted much about astronomy, all of a sudden?" And who's really the utter savage here, he asked himself quietly; he'd never have been able to pick out the next planet from the local sun against the starry sky, not without the ship's computer as a crutch.

The ancient Singer shrugged, gave Lando a saggy, toothless grin. "It is all there, Lord, in the Song of the Reflective Telescope, which detaileth all things in this system. Should it not be so?"

There was a long, long silence, during which the only thing accomplished was Vuffi Raa's computer-guided confirmation that Lando's "bright light in the heavens" was, indeed, Rafa V. "How many of these bloody chants do you know, anyway?"

The savage considered: "Many beyond counting, Lord. More than the fingers and toes of all my great-great ancestors and children. I would say approximately seven point six two three times ten to the fourth. Does this please thee, Lord?"

For a humble worshiper, the old boy was getting pretty sarcastic, Lando thought. "I suppose that last comes from the Song of Scientific Notation." He shook his head. He understood fully now why Gepta and Mer hadn't gone on this wild *falumba* chase themselves. It had nothing to do with conforming to ancient Toka legends. They simply wanted to stay sane.

The question now was, why did Vuffi Raa and Mohs need him?

"What now, Master? Do you want to go to Rafa V?"

"DON'T CALL ME MASTER!"

* * *

The relatively short jump of a few dozen million kilometers was blessedly uneventful for the captain and "crew" of the *Millennium Falcon*.

They hadn't started it at once. Vuffi Raa and Lando quizzed the elderly Mohs, had made him repeat and translate the appropriate stanzas of the appropriate Songs until they, too, were as certain as they could be, under the circumstances, that Rafa V was the place to find the Mindharp.

That is, if you were willing to place much confidence in an intermittently senile shaman mouthing rhymed and metered legends of an indeterminate age.

Lando spent the few hours of transit catching up on his sleep, while Mohs and Vuffi Raa carried on whatever passed for conversational small talk between them. The pilot's acceleration couch was infinitely more comfortable than the sleeping bag, and by the time Vuffi Raa woke him again, he felt halfway human. Downright cheerful, in fact. Or at least as cheerful as he ever—

SPANG!

Something struck the roof of the control cabin, hard.

"What in the eternal blue blazes was that?" Lando shouted. Behind him, the old man cringed, began gibbering to himself in a high-pitched, hysterical voice. Something about the wrath of—

SPENG!

This time, it was somewhere aft, near the engines. A yellow light winked on the control board. Vuffi Raa stabbed console buttons, his tentacles blurring with speed into near invisibility. "One moment, Master, while I—"

SPING! SPONG!

Red lights flickered now. There was the faint but definite whistle indicating loss of atmosphere. Lando swallowed hard. His ears popped as the pressure equalized, although that hadn't been his intention.

Something was striking the *Millennium Falcon* repeatedly and with great force. For some odd reason, the image of Constable Jandler (if that was really his name) flashed through Lando's mind. They were in close orbit over Rafa V, preparing to use the old Toka chants as a guide to selecting a landing site.

Vuffi Raa heeled the *Falcon* over so she could take whatever was hitting her on her better-armored underside, but they had already received at least minor damage.

SPUNG!

"In the name of the Galactic Center, what's *that*?" Lando hollered.

An unlikely object had wedged itself into the space between the cockpit transparency and a small communications antenna. It resembled nothing more than a fancy cut-glass plumber's helper, complete with handle and suction cup, but rendered in some crystalline substance reminiscent of Rafa orchard produce.

"I don't know, Master!"

Was that hysteria in the robot's voice? Wonderful, thought Lando.

The ship rolled, stabilized, and they were traveling in orbit on her side. The bombardment seemed to slacken off. The droid turned to Lando.

"It's an artifact of some kind, Master. Archaeoastronomers believe that Rafa V was the original home of the Sharu, the planet they evolved on. Mohs' Songs seem to agree with that. I suspect, Master, that we're seeing—and suffering—the remnants of their first attempts at spaceflight, objects launched by primitive rockets, others expelled by small spacecraft as they prepared to reenter atmosphere."

It made sense. Planetary orbits were always the richest fields in which to discover the leavings of primitive technology. There were probably cameras out there, used spacesuits, free-fall table scraps, all of them practically as good as the day they had been jettisoned—barring a little micrometeorite and radiation damage.

A thought came to him.

"Vuffi Raa, why didn't you just power the *Falcon*'s

shields up when we started taking hits? There's nothing out there the deflectors couldn't have handled, especially given our relative speeds in orbit."

Reading through the flight manual over and over again seemed to be doing him some good, Lando thought. Maybe if he watched the robot fly this machine long enough, he'd pick up the knack himself.

On the other hand, right now he could be aboard a luxury passenger liner, sipping a tall cool drink and shearing two-legged sheep.

"Why, I don't know, Master," came the reply. "I simply acted as quickly as I could. Brace yourself, everybody, we're going in!" The droid began punching console buttons again.

Rafa V—birthplace of the fabled Sharu or not—was not the favored planet for human colonization. There was atmosphere, the usual thick scattering of titanic multicolored buildings, and, most importantly, the ubiquitous life-orchards. But the place was just a trifle too cold, a trifle too dry, and Rafa IV, the planet they'd just come from, was moist and shirt-sleeve comfortable over a wide range of latitudes.

Here and there, according to their orbital survey and maps programmed into the *Falcon* at Teguta Lusat, lay small settlements, orchard-stations where a combination of Toka (native to the planet, as they were to all bodies in the system with sufficient resources), convicts, and government horticulturists harvested life-crystals, although on nowhere near the scale of Rafa IV.

No doubt in another hundred years or so, there would be towns, eventually cities other than those the Sharu had abandoned. But for now, there were a paltry few hundred individuals sprinkled over an entire planetary surface.

The colossal pyramid Mohs pointed them toward was at least a thousand kilometers from any contemporary outpost of civilization.

Vuffi Raa brought the *Falcon* to a gentle leaflike landing in a space between several ancient constructs at the foot of the pyramid that dwarfed even them. There were no convenient words to describe the building that now loomed over them. At least seven kilometers of it protruded above ground level. The *Falcon*'s various scanners had disclosed that it kept on going beneath the surface, but the depths exceeded the capabilities of her instruments. It was a literal mountain of smooth impervious plastic that served no discernible function.

The pyramid had five facets (not counting the bottom—wherever *that* was), the angles between each of them not particularly uniform, giving the gigantic construct an eerie, dangerous, lopsided look. Each face was a different brilliant color: magenta, apricot, mustard, aquamarine, turquoise, lavender.

Execrable taste, Lando thought, well deserving of cultural extinction.

There was no finishing ornament at the top; the sides simply came together in a peak sharp enough to give anyone who reached it a nasty puncture wound.

Not for the first time, Lando wondered who or what it was that had scared off creatures capable of creating such an edifice. He rummaged through the ship's chests and his own wardrobe looking for suitable clothing, settled finally on a light electrically heated parka, heavy trousers, micro-insulated gloves, and rugged boots with tough, synthetic soles. It was a measure of his uneasiness about the place that he broke long precedent, slinging a short, weighty, two-handed blaster over his shoulder and filling his pockets with extra power modules.

The weapon hung at his waist, muzzle swinging with his body when he moved.

Mohs flatly turned down the offer of additional warm clothing, joined the gambler and Vuffi Raa at the boarding ramp. Lando wondered if the old fellow wanted to add frostbite to the rest of his infirmities. If nothing else, they already made an impressive collection.

"Now, you're absolutely certain this is the place?"

Mohs nodded vigorously as the ramp lowered them and itself to ground level, unaffected by the cold as the angle beneath their feet steepened and a deep chill entered the belly of the ship. Air puffed out in visible vaporous clouds. They tramped down onto the dry-frozen soil.

"Master," Vuffi Raa admonished, "I trust you're carrying sufficient water. The humidity in this region does not quite reach two percent."

Lando slapped the gurgling plastic flasks tucked into the pockets of his parka. "Yes. And I brought a deck of card-chips, as well." He looked out over the barren surface of the planet. Fine reddish sand lapped like a frozen sea around the bases of the abandoned buildings. "Chances are we'll die of boredom before thirst gets to us."

Mohs turned, an odd look on his face as he watched Lando open a small panel at eye-level on one of the *Falcon*'s landing legs. The gambler pushed a sequence of buttons that started the boarding ramp groaning upward again into its recess under the ship's belly.

"Hast thou also the Key, Lord, the Key which—"

"What is this? Are you two seeing me off to summer camp or something?"

He led them out from beneath the ship, took a deep invigorating breath—and promptly froze the hairs in his nostrils. "Well, I can see why nobody much has staked a claim on this forsaken stretch of—"

"Master," Vuffi Raa clattered up beside him and tugged at the hem of his jacket. "Master, I don't like this, there's something—"

"I know, old junkyard, I can feel it, too."

The sky, a light greenish color, was cloudless. Nevertheless, somehow it impressed them all as gray, bleak, and overcast. And it was *cold*. The whine of Vuffi Raa's servos was clearly audible, a sign that perhaps his internal lubrication was thickening. Lando replaced the glove on the hand he'd used to retract the ramp, thrust it deeply into a warm pocket where the blaster swung.

"Master!"

Something went *zing!* and a short, stubby, wicked-looking arrow suddenly protruded from the seam between the robot's leg and body. In the next instant, a hailstorm of the primitive projectiles whistled toward them, bouncing off the *Falcon*'s hull, burying themselves in the sand at their feet. Vuffi Raa went down, looking like a five-legged pincushion. He didn't utter a word.

Curiously, not a single arrow struck either Lando or Mohs. The former swung his weapon up on its strap, panned it along the low dunes a few yards away. He felt a *slap!* and turned the blaster, staring at the muzzle orifice with disbelief.

An arrow had found its way straight down the bore, turning the gun into a potential bomb, should Lando touch the trigger. He tossed the dangerous thing away, began struggling with the fastenings of his coat to find the sting-beam. It wasn't much, but it was all—

"Stand where you are, '*Lord*'!" Mohs exclaimed, "If you resist, you will die before you draw another breath!"

The old man raised a hand. From behind the sand dunes, half a hundred Toka emerged, dressed as he was in nothing more than loincloths.

In his hands, each held a powerful crossbow, pointed directly at Lando.

TEN

So THIS WAS A GENUINE LIFE-ORCHARD.

The trees were a little odd, but nothing spectacular. In the wild grove perhaps five hundred of the things grew, in no particular pattern, yet each was of an identical size and spaced several meters from its nearest neighbor. The trunk was relatively ordinary, too—until one examined it closely and discovered that what appeared to be bark-covered wood was in fact a fibrous glassy pigmented stem approximately half a meter through and a couple of meters tall under the spreading branches.

The first oddity one noticed, however, was the root system. Each tree seemed to rest on a base, an irregular disk two meters across, like a toy tree in a model monorail set. Composed of the same substance as the trunk, the disk spread from the tree, forming a platform that curved abruptly downward at the edge and buried itself in the ground. The entire undersurface was covered with hair-fine glassy roots reaching downward perhaps a kilometer but spreading laterally only as far as the longest of the branches.

The branches, in some ways, reminded one of a cactus. At about average head height, they began to sprout from the trunk, departing at a right angle for a little distance (the lower the branch, the longer the distance, none exceeded the span of the root system), then turning straight upward. Outer branches—lower ones—had shorter vertical components. Inner ones had longer, so that the entire tree was somewhat conical in shape.

At the slender, tapering tip of each branch, a single, faceted, brilliant crystal grew, varying from fist-sized, on the outer branches, to tiny gems no bigger than pinheads. Each tree bore perhaps a thousand crystals. In the center, along the line of the trunk, one very tall, slender branch reached skyward like a communications antenna, unadorned by a crystal.

These trees were a little shorter, a little stockier than Lando had been led to believe was normal. Perhaps the milder climate of Rafa IV had something to do with that. It was hard to understand how anything could grow on Rafa V.

For grow they did, those trees—despite the fact that they were some odd cross between organic life and solid-state electronics. From some unknown spread of seeds, each orchard grew, every tree at the same rate. Remove a crystal from its branch tip—something which had to be done with a laser—and another would replace it within a year's time. Elsewhere in the Rafa System, Lando knew there were groves of trees no more than a hand's-width tall, others in which no tree stood less than ten or twelve meters. All bore crystals proportionate to the tree size. Some life-crystals, uselss for commercial purposes, were microscopic. Others were the size of Vuffi Raa's body.

The thought of Vuffi Raa caused Lando to stop thinking

about trees and reflect, instead, on how he'd gotten into this predicament.

Back at the ship, he'd turned in dismay to look at the little robot. Its red-lit eye was out; arrows stuck from nearly every chink and crevice of its body. A light clear fluid ran from many of the wounds, darkening the reddish soil around it.

Mohs strode up to him, no longer bent and stooped. He thrust out a hand, palm up.

"Give me the Key, *imposter*!"

Lando set his jaw. He didn't have much to lose, and he was mad—more at himself than anything else. He folded his arms across his chest, planted his feet in the sand, and grunted.

"The Key! It is not yours, it is ours! Give it to me!"

"Don't be silly, old fellow!"

Quite inexplicably, a look of dismay spread over Mohs' face. He dropped his hand to his side, turned to the other natives surrounding the pair in a heavily armed and dangerous-looking ring, and shrugged. He turned again to Lando.

"I say once more, you fake, you fraud, you, you . . ."

"If you do," said Lando, not understanding what was happening, but willing now to hope, "I'll just say something insulting. In fact, I think I will, anyway: your mother Sang off key." He nodded for emphasis.

Mohs took a step backward, aghast—whether at the magnitude of the insult or in surprise at the general turn of events, Lando couldn't tell.

Mohs turned once again to his people—and there's another problem, Lando thought idly: Mohs was from another planet. How was it that the locals seemed to know him and acknowledge his leadership?

Come to think of it, how had the ambush been set up in the first place?

The savages conferred for a while in their own language.

A decision appeared to have been made.

"You will come with us, imposter!" Mohs ordered. He started to walk off on a course paralleling the nearest face of the giant pyramid. Lando stood where he was.

"I will when the Core freezes over! *Owch!*" This last was due more to surprise than injury. A crossbow bolt had whistled past Lando's head, skinning an ear already made painful by the cold, striking the hull of the *Falcon*, and catching him on the rebound in the seat of his insulated pants. A pattern seemed to be emerging: they didn't want to kill Lando; they couldn't take the Key away without his consent (although Mohs had tried that back on Four, he reminded himself), but they could threaten and coerce him on other things.

They seemed to be pretty good at that.

He reached for his discarded blaster, intending to pull out the arrow and create a little mayhem before they shot him down. He hadn't moved a meter when another flight of arrows virtually buried the weapon, pinned it to the ground by its sling, trigger guard, and other apertures in the stock and fore end. So much for that idea.

As one, the fifty or so natives swung their weapons back on Lando.

"Okay, okay, I'm coming! Anybody think to call a cab?"

Two hours later, Lando wished it hadn't been a joke. They'd marched him for mile after endless mile, climbing over random, angular ruins, sloshing through deep-drifted sand, scrabbling through scrubby brush. His feet hurt and his legs ached and, no matter how high he turned his suit controls, he was still cold.

At last he stopped.

"All right, everybody, I've been a nice guy so far, but this is as far as I go. If you want the Key, you'll have to take it off my dead body. I'm not going another meter."

The silent natives who surrounded him looked to Mohs.

The old man nodded. They loosed a flight of arrows that plucked at his clothing, kicked sand up in his face, whistled mere angstrom units over his head. These fellows were impressive markspersons, Lando found himself thinking; I hope none of them gets the hiccups. He stood his ground again until they started shooting between his legs.

It wasn't worth the risk. He waited until they paused to reload, then began marching again.

What he had thought were crossbows had turned out to be something entirely different, some kind of spring-loaded contraption with hinged arms—which he'd mistaken for the limbs of a bow—that flailed forward, hurling the stubby arrows out through the front of the weapon. They didn't seem to need reloading every time they were fired. He guessed there were perhaps half a dozen projectiles stashed in a magazine hidden within the mechanism. The weapons weren't very powerful, as projectile throwers went, but the speed and accuracy with which they could be used made him realize he could die from a thousand pinpricks as easily as from a single blaster shot.

And a great deal more painfully.

They marched.

Another couple of hours went by. Lando wasn't sure exactly—he didn't want to look at his watch, because he didn't want to remind the natives that he had several items concealed beneath his winter clothes, notably his five-shot stingbeam. It would take a lot of figuring to get any good out of it in this situation, but it was something to fall back on, and it gave him a bit of hope.

Step after endless step. The country didn't vary much: something between desert and tundra, most of the space taken up with giant Sharu buildings. Sand, sand, and more sand. Occasional weeds. The clear, yet somehow foreboding sky. He worried about Vuffi Raa, hoped that robots die a swift and merciful death.

All during the long, pauseless ordeal, the Toka around him chanted, sometimes slowly, sometimes more rapidly.

And to his continuous annoyance, *never* in rhythm with the marching. This caused him to stumble awkwardly every now and again. He didn't know how the Toka mind worked, but he knew he didn't like it. They sang low-pitched Songs, they sang high-pitched Songs. They sang in harmony, disharmony, and counterpoint. They would be great to record—they had an endless repertoire.

At long last, the marching ended at a grove of life-crystal trees.

Mohs approached him.

"Imposter, hear me: we are forbidden to remove the holy Key from the Key bearer, even should the Bearer be a false one. You have somehow guessed this. Nor may we kill him who bears the Key, although we *have* killed the false Emissary, which makes us glad."

So *that* was it! Somehow Lando had gotten the idea that the Key Bearer and the Emissary were the same fellow, namely himself. Had he betrayed that belief to Mohs, setting up the debacle? He tried to recall what he'd said to Mohs on the subject, then realized it didn't make a bit of difference anyway—and besides, the old man was still talking.

"—let them do it themselves. Come with me!"

Lando followed him to a tree. Several of the other Toka handed their weapons to comrades, joined Mohs and Lando, and, between them, produced a loincloth.

By the time Lando decided to resist, it was too late. They forced him into a sitting position, bound him to the tree trunk by the waist, and used the same length of cloth to tie his hands behind him. They pushed back his hood, unfastened his jacket, and tore it rudely from him.

"Hey! Do you know what my tailor charged me for—now hold on a minute, that's going too far!"

Mohs had pulled off one of Lando's boots, bent to seize the other. When this was accomplished, the boots tossed aside near his discarded parka, they tore his tunic off, and the light shirt beneath it.

Then Mohs produced a knife.

"Now wait a blasted minute, here! You can't do that!"
He kicked at the old man until a pair of natives held his
ankles. He'd never believed in strong, silent heroes, and
since the only thing he had left to do was yell, he yelled.

He yelled the entire time it took Mohs to slit his trouser
legs, exposing bare skin to the chilling air.

"Now," said the ancient Singer, when he was satisfied
with Lando's disheveled condition. "All will notice that the
Key remains with the Bearer."

This was true. They'd taken it from his tunic and tucked
it into the dirty gray cloth about his waist. That had been
a scary moment—he'd held deathly sill so they wouldn't
clank it against the tiny beamer hidden beneath both loincloth and cummerbund.

"Now we shall wait. In Their own time, They will take
his life, either in the cold or through the tree. We shall then
return and claim the Key which is our rightful heritage. We
go."

They went.

As the sun sank behind the highly unnatural skyline,
shadows crept inexorably toward the helpless gambler, and
as they did, his heart sank at approximately the same rate
as the sun. He watched as small plants curled themselves
into little protective balls for the night. He watched as frost
formed on his toes. He watched as moisture in the ground
forced up the top layer of the soil on frozen ice columns.

Mostly, he watched his nice warm parka, tunic, boots
and socks gather frost of their own, not three meters beyond
his bound and helpless reach.

He began cursing, first through genuine anger at himself
and Mohs and Gepta and Mer, then simply in order to keep
warm. He cursed in his native tongue and in the dozen and
a half others he'd learned during a long and checkered
career. He cursed in three computer languages and the war-
bling *cheep* of a race of musical birds he'd once played
cards with—until it reminded him of the Toka.

He cursed the Toka all over again. And again. And again.

He woke up with a start!

And began cursing for no other reason than to stay awake. If he didn't, he would freeze to death.

ELEVEN

DEATHLY SILENCE.

Beneath a looming, monstrous, crustacean form resting on stilted legs, the twin pale moons of Rafa V picked out metallic reflections in the night-blackened sand. Shadows overlaid at different angles with slightly differing shades: the enormous double shadow of the *Millennium Falcon*, hundreds of tiny double shadows of stubby wooden projectiles buried in a fragile metal carapace and nearby soil.

Deathly silence and deadly cold.

Everywhere within sight of the *Falcon*, small, ground-hugging plants had rolled themselves into compact olive-colored balls in order to survive the frigid darkness. The air was dry, even drier than the daytime atmosphere. The subtlest sparkling of frost showed here and there, on half-frozen plantlife, on the crest of miniature dunes, on the rims of a thousand footprints that surrounded the ship, even on the tortured, tangled mess of chromium cables lying in a heap just outside the *Falcon*'s shadow.

Fluid still stained the sand for a short distance around the pitiable heap, slow and thick and gummy now, in the frozen quiet. Yet, a few inches beneath the grainy surface, there was movement. Pseudo-organisms, shiny and metallic, motelike, hovering at the edge of human visibility, stirred within the thickened fluid, migrated a millimeter at a time back toward the larger pseudo-organism they had tumbled from before dark.

Microscopic flagella beat languidly, laboriously. Yet, centimeter by centimeter, millions of the tiny objects swam what was to them enormous distances, back to where they belonged. In their wake, the fluid became thinner, more liquid, and withdrew after them, carrying minerals and trace metals from the soil with it.

The same two moons cast double shadows several kilometers away. Beneath a spread of glassy boughs, a figure huddled, trying to stay alive in the cold. Lando Calrissian was dying. As Vuffi Raa's life had run out into the sand, so he could feel his own life running out through his exposed skin into the frigid air, into the hungry sinister plant he was bound to.

Around him, if he'd cared to look, he might have seen the same small plants rolled up into the same small, heat-conserving spheres. He might have wished that he could do the same. But he was past all that, by now. From time to time he shivered, convulsions wracking his body, seeming to tighten the painful fibers around his waist, around his wrists, cutting off the circulation even further.

It was getting hard to think, and Lando didn't know whether the cold was causing that or the tree. It seemed important to figure it out. What had he heard about trees like this? That there was nothing free in the universe—that what the crystals gave to those who wore them, they had first taken from someone else. Were they taking from him now?

Most of all, it hurt. His naked feet felt as if they were

on fire. Even in the parched air, frost was forming on their tips, on the nails. How cold does tissue have to be before frost will form on it. Cold enough for gangrene?

Well, they weren't going to get him *that* easily! He nodded confirmation to himself, and only then noticed the tears that had run down his cheeks and frozen there. If he could still feel his feet—he wished he couldn't because the agony was as distracting as the cold itself—he ought to be able to feel his fingers. They were cold, too, but shielded from the air by his body, the little clothing they'd left him, and the tree.

The tree.

Its glassy trunk was like a block of ice at his back. Overhead, its strangely precise limbs showed a bit of transparency—or was it translucency?—where they crossed the moons.

He shook his head, and a pattern stopped. Dully, he tried to figure out what was missing. Had his heart stopped beating? He didn't think so. He was still breathing—only now that he was conscious of it, it became an effort, an added burden to keep on doing so. He wished he could forget about it, begin breathing automatically again.

That was it! Unconsciously, he'd been doing something with his hands, his fingers. Why did the tips of his fingers hurt? Were they frozen, like his toes? They shouldn't be— but "shouldn't" was a funny word: he *shouldn't* be there, trussed up to a tree that was eating his mind. He should be . . . should be . . . what should he be doing? Something about long corridors and beautiful women and . . . and . . . *cardchips*! What would he do with card-chips?

Trying to figure that one out, he didn't notice that his fingers had gone back to picking the fabric at his wrists, stripping the aged cloth one shredded fiber at a time.

Begin with a metal pentagon, approximately thirty centimeters across its longest dimension, seven or eight centimeters thick at the edges, perhaps twice that in the rounded center.

In the center, a lens, deep red, the size of a man's palm. And dark. Dark where it should be glowing softly, warmly. Dark as death itself.

Back at the edges, seams. On the other side of each seam, a tubular extension, joined every centimeter or so, tapering gracefully, each joint a little closer, a little finer than the one that preceded it. Sinuous, serpentine, and very, very highly polished, reflecting a curve-distorted picture of the frozen moons and cruel stars. Tangled now, heaped up and disheveled.

And at nearly every joint, at nearly every seam, a crude stubby brown pencil, rough and splintered, hundreds of them, jutting out at every conceivable angle. Where each arrow pierced the thin, fragile metal, a tiny pool of thick, transparent fluid welled. Some of it dripped off curved shining surfaces to the sand a few centimeters below.

Travel down the graceful, violated sinuosity, tapering, tapering, slimming impossibly. Approximately a meter from the torso seam, the tentacles branch again, into five delicate tapering fingers. Usually, these are held together so the tentacle seems to have a single, well-proportioned tip, concealing a tiny red optic in each "palm," replicas of the larger eye in the torso. Now they are splayed, whether in haphazard array or in the agonies of death, only the mechanically sentient can tell, and they are a taciturn, unsentimental lot, for the most part, and will not say what it feels like for a machine to die.

Perhaps, exactly like their creators, they don't know, will never know until they experience it themselves and can't relay the sensations to others. Perhaps it's just as large a mystery to them as it is to everybody else. Perhaps.

Each slender, dainty finger is divided into joints, precisely like the tentacles—fine, impossibly tiny joints, such as a watchmaker would create, looking through his loupe, trying to still the microscopic trembling of his hands. After a few centimeters, the fingers branch yet again—something absolutely *no one* ever notices. The joints continue marching, tapering, growing smaller and finer until they vanish from unaided vision—and continue.

Those subfingers, at their ends, are hair-fine, wire-slender . . . alloy strong. Their inner composition is just as sophisticated, just as complex as any other portion of the creature they belong to. Yet, unlike the pentagonal metal torso, unlike the sinuous jointed tentacles, unlike even the slender adroit fingers, they are too small to be seen, too fine to be hit with an arrow.

One of them stirs. It waves back and forth languidly a moment, living a life of its own. It coils and uncoils, testing itself. It stretches minutely, contracts minutely. It doubles back, wraps itself around the base of an intruding wooden object that had pierced the body above it.

It pulls.

There is a gentle, sucking noise. Slowly the arrow surrenders, sliding out, grating through tortured metal. The hair-fine subfinger plucks it out, casts it away. Elsewhere, other wirelike extensions perform similar tasks. And on the inside, where torn and dented metal protrudes in sharp triangular, ragged, toothlike edges, nearly microscopic flagellated motes begin pushing, thrusting, hammering the metal skin back into place, almost a molecule at a time.

"The Bantha is a shaggy beast, although it has no hair. . . . Its feathers are unique, at least, because they aren't there. . . . Hee, hee, hee, hee, hee!"

Lando began coughing uncontrollably, choking on his genius as a poet. He was disappointed. No one would ever get to hear his cleverness—although he couldn't quite remember why at the moment. Whatever it was, it made him sad, and he lapsed directly from laughter into sobs.

His fingers, highly trained and skillful at manipulating card-chips, coins, the entrances to other people's pockets, went right on thinking for themselves, picking at the rough-woven cloth that bound the wrists above them, threatening to cut off their circulation before they had quite finished their self-assigned task.

"The governor of Rafa Four is fat as he can be . . . with fuzzy crown and stubby limbs, he looks just like a . . . bee? Fee? Me? Thee? *Thee*! He looks just like thee, old man, he looks just lika thee!"

Behind Lando, between his body and the pseudoplant, a final fiber gave way. With something akin to shock, Lando jolted back to reality momentarily, surprised that he could move his wrist, almost sorry as warmth crawled back into his right hand and the pins-and-needles began.

Vuffi Raa had problems larger than pins-and-needles. His own fingers were free, now, where the primitive arrows had pinned them to the ground and punctured them. His joints would be stiff and uncooperative for some while to come—shoot a bullet through a hinge sometime and learn why—but he was already plucking the projectiles from his tentacles.

The congealed fluid in each wound was hardened, not by cold, this time, but deliberately, by design, protecting his incredibly delicate inner mechanisms. He was through reclaiming fluid from the sand. The traces of raw materials he'd picked up that way wouldn't serve him long: he'd require refuelling—something he'd only done once before in his long, long memory—perhaps even an unprecedented lubrication.

But he was alive.

Moreover, he was conscious, having the spare power, at last, to divert into consciousness. He had taken over the programmed simple-minded self-repair mechanisms, and the work was going at quadruple speed. He was beginning to feel good again, knowing that what he could do for others of his kind he could also do for himself.

The frozen desert saw the first faint glow of ruddy amber

from the lens set in his pentagonal torso, a luminescence vastly dimmer and less conspicuous than the moons above—another conscious decision.

His body stirred the sand around it, continued plucking arrows out and healing.

Lando Calrissian pondered one of the deep philosophical problems of all time. His right arm was completely free, but he didn't know why that was important. What had he intended to do with that arm?

Something about being cold.

Well, that was silly: he wasn't cold at all. He was nice and warm. Nice and rosy warm. The warmth spread from his toasty feet, up through his legs, into his body, out through his shoulders. His ears were warmest of all. They were practically on fire.

Fire!

He looked around him. It was smoky enough for a fire. The grove where he sat so warmly comfortable seemed to be full of haze. Someone hadn't opened the damper on the fireplace, evidently. Well, he'd just have to get up in a few minutes and do it himself. Couldn't trust anybody these days, even with so simple a task as tending a—

Fire!

Something about a gun! Now what in the blazes would he do with a gun if he had one? There was nothing to shoot here, nothing to fight, nothing to eat, even if he'd been the wild-game type, which he wasn't. Besides, they'd plugged his gun up with an arrow. Devilishly good shots, those . . . those . . .

Now *who* had been that good a shot, shooting?

Shooting?

What did *that* have to do with anything? He'd been going to tend the fire, hadn't he? Well, no time like the—he tried to sit up. Great Galactic Core, he thought, I'm paralyzed from the waist down! No—I was simply careless putting on my pants and looped the belt around this . . . this . . .

With sudden, momentary clarity, he reached into his cummerbund, extracted his five-shot stingbeam pistol, flipped off the thumb-safety, and *fired*. The rough cloth fell from his waist. Almost in panic, he rolled away from the life-tree, and had to restrain himself from wasting his remaining four shots on the thing that had been sucking his brains away.

It cost him. Every bone, every muscle in his body, every square inch of his skin was in agony. Each movement threatened to shatter him or tear him. All he really wanted to do was go back to sleep. All he really wanted to do was rest. That was it: he knew he had other things to do, but he could rest up, first. Get warm again—not really sleep, just close his eyes and—

Nearly shrieking defiance—at what he was never afterward able to say—he rolled, crawled, pushed himself along the ground, inflicting new pains with every centimeter of progress. At least he reached the heap of clothing Mohs and his bravos had stripped from him, nearly dived into the parka, and turned the thermoknob to Emergency Full.

And the agony *really* began.

There wasn't much he could do about his pants. They'd been sliced open from cuff to crotch—Lando remembered the knife, seemingly made from a life-crystal. The abandoned loincloth still clung to his waist. With stiff fingers, he spread it out, tore it into strips, wrapped the strips around his legs, and tied them at strategic points to hold his trousers together.

Bundled up in the parka, he put the gloves on next. The stingbeam was small enough to conceal inside the right glove so that he could shoot in a hurry if he needed to. The little weapon was blessedly warm from the one shot he'd expended.

Time to think about standing up. Should he take the parka off, replace his undershirt and tunic? It would be in better taste, but somehow that didn't seem to matter right now. Oh, yes! He'd almost forgotten about his boots and socks.

When he got around to examining his feet, he almost wished he hadn't. He was going to miss those toes, and regeneration was a long, fairly painful process. Oh, well, to paraphrase an old, old saying, it beat the hell out of having to regenerate new feet. With great tenderness, he pulled his socks on—being careful to dump as much sand out of them as possible—and, over those, his boots.

How the dickens was he going to stand up? He didn't dare approach one of the deadly trees close enough to lean against it. He rolled over on his side, pulled his knees up, rolled up onto them.

It felt as though someone had clamped his feet in a vise and was tightening it. He told himself that at least he was alive enough to feel pain. Somehow that didn't cheer him much. He told himself that at least he had his mind back, could think, wasn't going to be a drooling vegetable.

He clambered to his feet, forced himself to walk around.

So this was a genuine life-orchard. It had bloody well nearly been a death orchard, he thought. Wouldn't Mohs be surprised, come morning, to find his victim gone, and along with him—

The Key!

He felt beneath his cummerbund. Even through both gloves and coat, he couldn't mistake the lumpy weirdness of the artifact. Well, *that* was going to upset the old man. Lando chuckled to himself.

The thought came to him that perhaps he was being watched. Well, *let* them watch! The stingbeam didn't have an orifice like a blaster, its muzzle was a pole-piece, more like a thick, stubby, rounded antenna than anything else. He was alive, intelligent, on his feet—he was going back to the *Falcon* for a hot cup of—

Vuffi Raa!

It had been one monster of a day! He'd nearly been killed, certainly been hijacked, and lost his best friend. No, he wasn't ashamed to say it: the little droid had been a better, more loyal friend to him than any he'd ever had before. He was going to miss the little guy.

Now, which way was the *Falcon*? Simple: just follow the tracks, which, with the double portion of moonlight and the dry, still atmosphere, were still plainly visible in the sand.

He took a step.

LANDO CALRISSIAN!

Before he realized it, the glove was off his right hand, the stingbeam pointed aloft. Overhead, a repulsor-vehicle hovered, bright with running lights, a searchbeam shining down on him and illuminating the entire grove.

It settled to the ground.

"Drop your weapon," a familiar voice said over the loudhailer, *"and put your hands over your head!"* Lando didn't move.

Nor did he move when four constabulary troopers, their armor glinting in the moonlight, jogged up beside him, took his gun away, and held their own weapons leveled at his chest.

Captain Jandler—if that was his name—had rendered his own visor transparent, this time. He strutted over from the hovercar.

"Well, Captain Calrissian, we meet again. As soon as we've taken care of you, we'll recover your vessel and get that cargo back to its rightful owners. If you thought you were in trouble before... By the way, you have something else we want. Where is it?"

"Where is what?" said Lando between gritted teeth.

"The Sharu artifact. The Key the governor gave you. Where is it?"

"Come and get it, thug!"

"All right, men, we're going to do it the hard way. Search him. Strip that clothing off and search him!"

TWELVE

THUNDER BOOMED OVERHEAD!

Bathed in a glorious dawn that hadn't yet reached the ground beneath it, the *Millennium Falcon* roared down upon a constabulary detachment frozen with confusion and surprise, and stood hovering a dozen meters over their heads.

Lando seized Guard-Captain Jandler's weapon muzzle, swung it aside, and kicked the hapless policeman. Jandler sank with a moan to his knees, eyes crossed beneath his helmet visor, and, with a preoccupied gurgle, collapsed onto his face. Lando resisted the urge to kick him again, someplace more breakable.

Two things happened at the same time: one of the other police officers leveled his blaster at the gambler, a finger whitening inside his gauntlet on the trigger. Roiled dirt and fire spurted up into a wall ahead of him as a turret on the *Falcon* spat energy down at him. He dropped his gun and raised his hands unbidden, as did two of his comrades. They were out of the game.

The fourth wasn't giving up so easily. He seized the opportunity to dash for the repulsor-cruiser where a heavy beamer was mounted on the transom. Before he'd taken three hurried steps, the starship's turret pivoted, a second energy bolt lashed down from above, and the police cruiser heaved upward from the ground, fell back in flaming wreckage. Smoke poured from the ruined vehicle into the rapidly lightening sky.

Keeping a wary eye on Jandler, Lando sat down heavily himself, wondering where all his vim and vigor had come from all of a sudden. And where it had gone just as abruptly. The *Falcon* settled, its active turret still aimed at the policemen. Lando noticed the guard-captain's heavy blaster, lying in the sand a few inches from his rag-wrapped knee, picked it up and rested it in his lap.

The *Falcon*'s long, broad boarding ramp creaked down slowly. After a while there was a flash and twinkle at the dark, inner end of the passage. Vuffi Raa came slither-marching down to the ground, his posture and movements conveying somehow that he was rather pleased with himself—although he looked a bit worse for the previous evening's wear.

"Master! I'm gratified to see you're still alive. I feared I wouldn't get here in time, but I see you've taken care of nearly everything yourself already."

The gambler grinned wearily, accepted the proffered tentacle. "I'm gratified myself, considering some of the alternatives. But you look like you've been out in a meteor shower! Or is that the latest robot fashion you're wearing?"

From eye lens to manipulator tips, the little droid was covered with small, rounded dents. Where they overlapped his joints—which was practically everywhere—his movements were a little stiff and uncertain, and he sounded, when he replied, just the slightest bit self-conscious.

"Yes, well, these arrow wounds are healing, Master. In not too many days I'll be quite myself again. But you have suffered damage which will not be repaired so quickly. We must get you into the ship, where I can administer—"

"Hold it." Grunting, Lando hauled on Vuffi Raa's tentacle, pulled himself onto his knees, and, placing a palm firmly in the middle of the little robot's lens, pressed himself upward, to his feet. He swayed a little, but he was vertical— and still had the blaster pointed straight at the constabulary contingent.

Meanwhile, Captain Jandler was beginning to do some grunting of his own. He rolled over, tears welling from his eyes and dripping on the inside of his visor, shook his head from side to side, and lay there, still doubled up.

"We'll administer to me later, old pencil-sharpener. First we're going to 'administer' to our military friend, here. He seems to be among the living, again, although how long . . ."

Lando offered the blaster to the droid, glancing significantly at the four undamaged troopers. "While I'm attending to Jandler, I don't suppose you could . . ."

"Hold them at bay? I'm afraid not, Master. I cannot threaten a living being with bodily harm. Sorry."

"Well, I'm not complaining, not anymore. I'll just have to keep an eye on them myself. But I am curious: how was it that, ten minutes ago, you could—"

"Use the *Millennium Falcon*'s armament to keep them from attacking you?"

"And to do that demolition job on the police cruiser. Neat, but a little outside your specialties, wouldn't you say?"

Lando approached the semiconscious guard-captain, toed him not too roughly in the armored ribs. "All right, time to rise and shine! We've got a little talking to do!"

Vuffi Raa shambled up beside the gambler. "Master, I can watch the troopers for you, and they needn't know I can't initiate force against them." The little robot continued in a louder voice, intended for a broader audience, "If one of them so much as twitches an earlobe, we'll burn him off at the kneecaps!"

Lando chuckled, "Yeah, right up to the armpits! Just be sure"—he whispered to Vuffi Raa—"that you don't compromise yourself into a nervous breakdown." Then he added, more loudly, "I said get up, you!"

Jandler stirred, did some more groaning, rolled over, and sat up painfully. Wincing, he took off his helmet and wiped sweat from his face.

"Calrissian, you just plain don't fight fair, do you?"

Lando aimed the confiscated blaster at its former owner's nose. "I don't like to fight at all. When I have to, I try to get it over with as quickly and neatly as possible. Now, *WHAT IN THE BLAZES IS THIS ALL ABOUT?*"

Jandler, his troopers, even Vuffi Raa jumped a little at this outburst. The police leader blinked, considered, then shook his head and sighed.

"Okay, Calrissian—I wish to perdition I knew! I've been sent on more crazy errands in the last couple of days than in my whole career, up until now: your hotel room, the Spaceman's Rest, the spaceport, and now this. It puts a man in mind of retiring early, pension or not. What do *you* know about it?"

Lando squatted down on his haunches, keeping the blaster centered on Jandler. "I hate like the devil to steal your line, Captain, but *I'm* asking the questions, here. Tell me, exactly where—rather, from whom—did you receive your orders, if one may ask?"

Jandler glanced quickly at his men, then back to Lando, and licked his lips. "Where do you think? From that fat son-of-a-"

"Captain!" shouted one of the cops, "you can't—"

"The Entropy I can't! Do you think that overstuffed chair-warmer gives a nit in a nova what happens to any of us? All he cares about is that Sharu doohicky, and if we come back without it, we might as well not come back! Well, I—"

"You mean this?" Lando drew the Key from his waist-band. It gleamed in the early morning sunlight and, if anything, seemed more disorienting than before.

Lando could see the guard-captain calculating whether

it was worth the risk jumping for it. He looked from the Key to his former blaster muzzle, across to Lando, up at Vuffi Raa, then back to the Key again. Finally, he shrugged.

"Let him get it for himself!" Jandler decided out loud. "Is there any way my men and I can get out of this alive, Captain Calrissian? I won't give you those hull-scrapings about 'just following orders again'—only, well, I'm not too fond of the idea of dying, just now. Especially since I seem destined to taste the fruits of civilian life for a while."

Lando turned, winked at Vuffi Raa, and looked back at Jandler.

"Well, old Constable, you people do seem to present us with a problem. I'm impressed with your change of heart, but insufficiently so to be too happy about your breathing down my neck while I'm on this planet. Giving you all the Big Push would seem to be the answer—"

He held up a hand.

"—But I am highly disinclined in that direction, believe me. As you know, I am a gambler by profession, certainly no killer. I live by my wits, not by the gun, however useful the things may prove to be at times. If we can think of a way to let things work out for everybody, I'll certainly cooperate."

Jandler grinned, scratched his head. His men, a few yards away, seemed to relax a few notches as well.

"Now, Captain Jandler," said Lando, "this is what I think we'll do..."

The idea worked out better than Lando had expected.

Aboard the *Millennium Falcon*, there were several tough, inflatable life-bubbles that could be jettisoned, with air and other short-term supplies. A man could live inside one for several days in moderate discomfort. They weren't much use if something went wrong in interstellar space, but, in the neighborhood of a solar system—where most accidents happen anyway—they could keep one alive until assistance, summoned by an automatic radio beacon, arrived.

Lando's original plan was to haul the constabulary contingent out a few astronomical units and abandon them in space. They'd be out of his and Vuffi Raa's figurative hair for a few days, and yet live to tell their grandchildren about the experience. Happy ending all around.

The little droid made it happier.

"Well, Master, that takes care of that. I believe the gentlemen can go aboard now." He was exiting a hatch in the side of a powered interplanetary cargo barge, large, dark, and rusty, in which the police team had originally traveled to Rafa V. The humble vessel's presence had helped Vuffi Raa to locate Lando in the nick of time.

Lando transferred the blaster to his left hand, extended his right to the constabulary boss. "I suppose this is farewell, then, old bluecoat. I trust you and your comrades will enjoy the trip."

Jandler grinned. "It beats a beam in the eye from a hot laser, Captain Calrissian—"

"Call me Lando, nobody else seems to be able to do it."

"Lando, then. And when we get there, none of us will be in any particular hurry to report, *will we*, *guys*?" This last had a bit of an edge to it. The other four policemen quickly assumed a what? who, me? expression, and Lando trusted Jandler to keep them all in line. Not that it mattered. The plan was perfect.

The officers trooped aboard. Lando waved, then watched Vuffi Raa weld the hatch shut behind them.

"Thirty seconds, Master."

"Very well, let's get back out of the way."

Slowly, gently, with impossible grace, the ungainly tub of a spaceship lifted from the sand, guided by a program Vuffi Raa had punched into its miniscule electronic mind. Lando glimpsed the fused and blackened end of a communications antenna, one of three the little droid had ruined. For the duration of its trip, the barge would be out of contact with the rest of the Rafa System. It would take the vessel a week to reach Rafa XI, last and least planet of the colony, a bleak ball of slush circling in the dark.

A considerable research installation had been built there, and a fairly impressive helium refinery.

"You didn't forget the torches, did you?"

"*Please*, Master, it was difficult making myself do it, don't rub it in."

"Oh, very well. But sabotaging the ship's controls was *your* idea, I'll remind you. The cops can't alter the taped course, and they can't communicate with anyone until they're close enough to do it with flashlights out the viewports. You did send along that Oseon brandy, I trust?"

"Yes, Master, and those . . . those . . ."

"Holocassettes? Absolutely imperative, old gumball machine. The scenery where they're going is remarkably boring." He gave a final salute as the barge lifted through a rack of rare, high cirrus clouds and disappeared.

Vuffi Raa said nothing. In truth, he was rather proud of his master for sparing the men's lives, and especially for parting with them under somewhat cordial circumstances. Perhaps humans—this one in particular, at least—weren't such a bad lot, after all.

"All right," Lando said, breaking into the robot's reverie, "let's get moving ourselves. We've got to find the Toka. I'm going to kill that buzzard-necked Mohs if it's the last thing I ever do!"

The first thing they had done, after sending off the constabulary contingent, was to attend to Lando's wounds. Frostbite—of which he had been plentifully supplied by the previous evening's adventure—is no minor matter, can be as serious as a blastershot under some circumstances, and, even with all the facilities of modern medicine, can lead to gangrene in a matter of hours.

The *Millennium Falcon* did not provide all the facilities of modern medicine. In a locker, Vuffi Raa discovered a portable gel-bath, miniature version of the large, full-body devices used to heal serious wounds. It would fit Lando's feet nicely. He unfolded it in the common room and slid it under the gametable where Lando was considering a problem in Moebius chess.

Or appeared to be.

"Dash it all, Vuffi Raa, where would *you* be, on this planet, if you were an ancient savage with an angry outworlder after you?"

"I couldn't say, Master, the inscrutabilities of the organic mind—"

"Nonsense, old android. Your mind is every bit as organic as—"

"*Please*, Master, I have done nothing to deserve insult. If you truly wish, I will consider the problem you have just posed." Silence, then: "Why do you suppose he had us land the *Falcon* near that giant pyramid, Master?"

Lando gave up on the game, slapped the OFF switch, and watched the weird serpentine playing board fade and vanish from the tabletop.

"I've been wondering about that, myself. It's much the largest building on the planet—perhaps in the system, which would make it the largest in the entire galaxy, I'm sure. On the other hand, the Sharu—now *there* are some inscrutable minds for you—the Sharu may have used it to store potatoes."

"Or the Mindharp."

"Yes, although I'd venture that if the Mindharp were simply a device to tell the Toka to run and fetch their masters' pipe and slippers, it wouldn't deserve quite so august a resting place. However, one thing is certain: it *is* where that scoundrel Mohs met up with his savage cohorts. As such—"

"As such," Vuffi Raa ventured, "it may be a wonderful place to get ambushed—again. Hold still, please, Master, while I tape your ears."

"Leave my ears out of this, you mechanical menace, they were fine before."

"Master, please! I am programmed to—"

"All right, all right! Then limber up your piloting appendages. We're headed for that pyramid again. Only this time, I'm carrying *two* heavy blasters—and an umbrella to keep arrows out of the muzzles."

Mohs wasn't hard to find. When the *Millennium Falcon* arrived, he was sitting on a sand dune in the shadow of the pyramid, smoking a lizard.

THIRTEEN

"Twice have I doubted thee, O Lord, yea, even as twice hast thou proved me in error! Kill now thy miserable excuse for a servant, that he may disgrace thee no further!"

The fire, built of twigs and leaves in a scooped-out hollow in the ubiquitous reddish sand of Rafa V, was no larger than a teacup. It failed to warm Lando although he sat cross-legged not more than two feet away, trying to avoid noxious fumes rising from a branch that sported a small, disgusting reptile skewered neatly from end to end.

An ugly way to die, the gambler thought, even for a lizard. And it made an even uglier lunch.

"Look, Mohs, see me about that sometime when I'm not so tired. I may surprise you and take you up on the offer. In the meantime, are you still interested in trying to use the Key?"

"Of a certainty, Lord! Too long have my people, the wretched Toka, suffered under the tyrannical thumb of the—"

"Save it for the union meeting, Singer. All I want to know is where to put this thing. If somebody—your people, for instance—benefits, and somebody else loses as a result, well, that's no paint off my hull, I can assure you."

Secretly, the amateur star-captain was thoroughly enjoying the chance to use what he imagined was tough-sounding spacefaring jargon. Now that he'd had a hot meal, plenty of coffeine, and was wearing a fresh change of clean, undamaged clothes, he felt downright jaunty, even considering the miserable night he'd spent in the life-orchard.

"I don't give a hiccup out the airlock, even if *Gepta* benefits, as long as I get out of this confounded system with a full cargo and a whole skin—not necessarily in that order, mind you."

Mohs had started a little at the mention of the sorcerer's name. Now he positively reeled, managing to wring his bony hands at the same time. "O Lord, thy servant knoweth full well that thou sayest these cynical things only as a test of my faith, fortitude, and other virtues—"

"Which are too microscopic to be mentioned."

"—which are too microscopic to mention, as thou sayest, Lord. Yet, wouldst thou mind very much not making such vile, blasphemous, and mercenary utterances in the mortal presence of thy humble servant? It causeth unease."

"Oh it does, does it?"

Lando glanced back over his shoulder. He was pretty sure that at least half of the old man's "unease" derived from the imposing presence of the *Millennium Falcon* about fifty meters away across a clear expanse of sand, her full batteries trained in a protective circle to prevent a reenactment of the earlier ambush. In an inner pocket of his parka, her captain carried a transponder that kept the *Falcon*'s guns from sweeping within a couple of degrees of whoever wore it. This was a necessary precaution because Vuffi Raa was not at Battle Stations, inside.

He was programmed against it.

Somewhere back along the line, Lando had ceased resenting the little robot's programmed pacifism, and simply begun planning around it. In the righthand outside slash pocket of his parka, he carried a second device with which he could trigger every weapon aboard his ship. Vuffi Raa could handle opening the boarding ramp as Lando ran for it, if anything went wrong. It wasn't against his built-in ethics to *save* a life. In fact, the droid had proved himself quite useful in that department already.

But to the problem at hand.

"Okay, old theologue, we'll change the subject: How did you know we had survived this morning, and why did you wait for us here, when you knew how sore I'd be about last night?"

Lando wanted to move back from the fire. About a thousand meters would do nicely. The cooking reptile, presently hovering somewhere between second-degree blistering and third-degree charring, smelled exactly like . . . like . . . well, he'd smelled more appetizing things attached to starship hulls while he was melting them off with live steam. Nonetheless, even the idea of the fire was warming; he hadn't felt really comfortable since he'd landed on that stupid clot of sand, not even aboard skip.

The elderly Singer opened his mouth. "Lord—"

"MASTER, HUMAN FORMS ARE MOVING BEHIND THOSE DUNES OVER THERE."

Mohs *jumped* at least a meter. The little droid's voice had come amplified through the ship's external loudhailers.

"Thanks, old cogwheel." Lando answered in a normal tone. *Millennium Falcon* had excellent hearing, and so did Vuffi Raa. He chuckled as the antique shaman regained his dignity.

"THEY APPEAR TO BE CARRYING THOSE CROSS-BOW THINGS, MASTER."

"Mohs," the gambler said evenly, "I'm going to give you just thirty seconds to send your people away, and if they're not gone by then, you're going to swap places with that poor uncomfortable creature you're cooking. I ought to turn you in to the ISPCA—or at least the Epicures Club."

The Singer slowly cranked himself into a standing position, rattled off a few discordant stanzas—probably the

Song of Strategic Withdrawal, Lando thought—then he sat again, turned the lizard on its stick, and addressed Lando.

"I have told them to depart, Lord. They came only for your protection. Now, if thy servant may have a few moments in which to fortify himself and attend to bodily needs, then we shall go to a place I know . . . where the Key may be used."

He seized the lizard by its head, pulled backward in a peeling motion, and tore it off the stick.

"Good heavens," Lando cried, gulping to control his upper gastrointestinal tract, "are you going to eat that thing?"

Fifteen minutes later, they were standing at the base of the pyramid. Even tilted backward as the wall before them was, it seemed to loom over them like some fantastic, infinitely high cliff, threatening to topple and bury them at any instant.

Vuffi Raa, having locked the spaceship up securely, joined them. The Toka Singer cast around, seeming to look for something recognizable on what appeared to be a featureless magenta wall. Finally, he stopped and pointed.

"*There*," he said with finality, "about a meter downward, Lord." He folded his arms.

Lando rolled his eyes in exasperation. "Well, don't look at me. I'm the Key Bearer. *You're* the peon. You want a shovel, or will you perform this ceremony by hand?"

The old Toka was aghast. "*Me*, Lord? I am Singer of the—"

"One moment, gentlebeings," the robot said. "I can have it done before the two of you are finished arguing about it."

With that, his tentacles became a blur of motion. He resembled a shiny circular saw blade with a glowing red center. Sand poured upward on a wake behind him like an absurd dry fountain, and he was, as he had promised, soon finished.

"Escargot and Entropy!" Lando swore, struck by what

he saw where Vuffi Raa had dug. Mohs was startled into silence, fell to his knees and began chanting in a low, whimpery tone.

It shouldn't have been possible. Draw a line around your hand and rout out the material within the outline to a depth of approximately a centimeter. It can be done, and easily.

Now try it with the blade of an eggbeater. The human hand is, in its simplest representation, a two-dimensional form. Something requiring three dimensions can't be represented in the same way, not including its essential element—its three-dimensionality. Not unless that object is a Sharu artifact, and the people doing the bas relief are the Sharu themselves.

In some ways, it was rather as if the wall were transparent—which it was not—and the molded impression of the Key were buried yet visible inside it. But that wasn't truly the case. In another way, it was like seeing the Key itself, inside out, glued to the side of the pyramid—except that the "image" (or whatever it was) neither protruded from the surface nor was inset into it. The whole thing looked just as preposterous, just as impossible, as the Key itself, only more so.

And it hurt the eyes in just the same way.

Lando stepped back, blinked, and shook his head to uncross his eyes.

"All right, Mohs, suppose you tell us exactly what you know—what your Songs have to say, if anything—about what we're seeing and what happens if we use the Key in it."

The old man hummed a little to himself, at first as if to get the right pitch, then as if he knew the data only by rote and had to find the right place before he could start properly.

"This is the Great Lock, Lord. For generations uncounted, no Toka—no, nor any interloping stranger from the stars—has entered into the least of the many sacred shrines They left behind."

"Marvelous. We already knew that."

"Ah, yes, Lord, but now it is as it has been told: we shall enter, *without entering*. We shall walk the hallowed halls and yet they shall not echo to our feet. We shall travel to their farthest corners without going anywhere. We shall dream, therein, without sleeping, and know without learning. And, in due course and in Their time, we shall discover the Harp of the Mind; setting free the Harp, we shall set free the—"

"All right, all right. Politics again. Let me think this over a minute." He kicked experimentally against the bottom edge of the pyramid where it showed above the ground. There was no sound, no sensation of impact. It was like kicking at water or fine dust. "Vuffi Raa?"

"Yes, Master?"

"Don't call me master. What do *you* think about all this interloping business?" He took the Key from his pocket, turned it over in his hand, and thrust it back in his pocket.

"I think I'm long overdue for a lube job, Master, and would just as soon go home and—"

"I thought your lubricated areas were permanently sealed."

Was that a sheepish look in the droid's single eye? "Yes, Master, although I *did* get rather badly punctured and lost a good deal of...oh, I *can't* see any alternative to using the Key as Mohs suggests, Master. Much as I would like to."

Lando laughed. "I don't much like this enter-without-entering, sleep-without-dreaming stuff myself, truth to tell. Look here, Mohs, what else have you got for us—in plain language."

For the first time, the old man appeared to be uncomfortable on Rafa V. He had goosebumps all over him, and was shivering with the cold—or something else.

"That is all that is known to the Toka, O Lord. It is all that the Song hath to tell. Thy humble and obedient servant confesseth, in his unworthy manner, that, were I thee, I would consider departing this place without using the Key. All those numberless generations, waiting, waiting...Why me, Lord? Why in my time?"

"Congratulations, Mohs, you've just joined the ranks of some great historical figures. That's what *they* wanted to know, and usually in about the same miserable desperate tone of voice."

Again, Lando extracted the Key, looked it over grimly. "Well, there's no time like the present. Keep your eye open, Vuffi Raa. Mohs, what do your Songs say about using this thing?" He suppressed a shudder.

The old man gave a highly articulate shrug.

"That's what I like," Lando said, "help when I really need it. Here goes nothing!"

Which is precisely what happened. Lando pressed the Key against the lock in a position and at an angle that seemed most likely. It was a little like putting a ship in a bottle—at least it seemed that way at first. Then, in a manner that defied the eye and turned the stomach, the Key was in the Lock.

The sun shone. The wind blew. The sand lay on the ground.

Lando looked at Mohs, who still had some of his shrug left. He used it. The gambler looked at Vuffi Raa. Vuffi Raa looked back at him. The robot and the elderly shaman exchanged glances. They both looked at Lando.

"Well, Mohs, I realize you've had breakfast, or whatever you call it, but I could use another bite. This seems to be a bust. What say we repair to the ship and—Vuffi Raa?"

As he had spoken to the old man, he'd turned to look at the robot.

Vuffi Raa had vanished.

"Mohs, did you see that—Mohs?"

The instant Mohs was out of Lando's field of view, *he* had disappeared, exactly like the droid, without a sound, without a movement.

The sun shone. The wind blew. The sand lay on the ground.

FOURTEEN

Lando Calrissian was not, ordinarily, a physically demonstrative young man. His livelihood and well-being depended on dexterity and control, the subtle, quick manipulation of delicate objects, the employment of fine and shaded judgment.

He smashed a fist into the pyramid wall.

And reeled with surprise. Where, before, contact with the building had been much like ducking one's head into a stiff wind—elusive but unquestionably real—now the experience had taken on the aspect of fantasy.

His hand passed into the wall and disappeared as if the structure were a hologram. He withdrew the hand, looked it over, flexed it. He inspected the wall without touching it: the material itself was featureless, seemingly impervious to time, weather, the puny scratching and chipping of man. Yet there was a fine patina of dust, a film of oil or grease that seemed to coat everything within the planet's atmosphere. Lando could plainly see a single fine hair, neither his own nor one of Mohs—perhaps that of some animal that had wandered by or which had been borne on the wind until it stuck here.

He thrust his hand into the solid-looking wall again. Again it disappeared up to the wrist. He stepped forward until he lost sight of his elbow, shuddered, backed away. And, again, his hand, his arm, were intact, unharmed.

Lando Calrissian was nothing if not a cautious individual. Someone else might have plunged through the wall in pursuit of Vuffi Raa and Mohs, for it was clearly where they'd gone. But to what fate? If your best friend zipped from sight into a trapdoor in the floor, would you follow him onto the steel spikes below?

Lando pushed his hand into the wall again, meeting no more resistance than before. It was as if the wall weren't there—except as far as the eyes were concerned. He closed his own, and felt around. There wasn't enough breeze outside that he could tell about the wall's effect on air currents. The temperature felt the same. He was free to wiggle his fingers, clench and unclench his fist. He snapped his fingers, felt the snap—but couldn't hear it outside the wall.

Thrusting in a second hand, he felt the first. Both felt quite normal. He clapped them, feeling the sensation, missing the usually resultant noise. Odd. He placed his right hand around his left wrist, slid the hand slowly up the arm until it reappeared, much like a hand and arm emerging from water—except that this surface was vertical. He stooped, picked up a handful of sand, reinserted his arms, poured sand from one hand to the other.

He pulled his arms out, threw the sand away...

...and stepped through the wall.

Sometimes you have to take a gamble.

He hadn't thought of that before.

Old man Mohs, ancient and revered High Singer of the Rafa Toka, had been leaning against the pyramid wall when the Key-Bearer inserted the Key. Suddenly, it had been as if the wall weren't there, and, in the short fall into darkness that resulted, his garment had nearly been lost.

All his long, long life, Mohs had put up with the chilly draft that found its way beneath the simple wraparound. Now, even in the darkness, even in this terrifying, holy place, it had occurred to him that he could take a long free end of the cloth, tuck it up between his legs, and eliminate the draft.

Why hadn't he thought of that before? Why hadn't anybody else among his people? He found himself thinking cynically that the little piece of information alone was worth a hundred silly Songs about—no! That's blasphemy! He cringed, trying to peer into the utter darkness around him, fearful of . . . of . . . what?

He thought about that.

He seemed to be doing a *lot* of thinking in the past few minutes.

Finally, he decided—in what may have been the first real decision he'd ever made for himself—to wait until his eyes adjusted. He sat—on some firm, resilient surface— enjoying his new-found warmth.

And the new-found working of his mind.

It had been hours!

Four hours, twenty-three minutes, fifty-five seconds, to be precise, by Vuffi Raa's built-in chronometer. He never had to see the time, he simply knew. The trouble with built-in faculties, he reflected, such as being able to pilot a starship, for example, is that they denied or dulled the urge to acquire new ones for oneself. Better to be like a human being, he thought, without innate programming, with the ability and necessity—

A human being? What was he thinking?

He'd been approximately—no, exactly—seventeen centimeters from touching it with his nearest tentacle, and yet, when Lando had activated the Key, suddenly, he, Vuffi Raa, was here (wherever here was) on the other side.

Five hours, twenty-nine minutes, thirty-one seconds.

Exactly *what* here was, Vuffi Raa thought rather ungrammatically, was a good question in itself. He'd felt strangely isolated, lonely for quite a while, and, oddly, that feeling had preoccupied him so thoroughly that he'd failed to examine his surroundings with much enthusiasm. The feeling hadn't gone away, it had gotten worse, much worse. Now, it was necessary to investigate, if only to take his badly shaken mind off his emotions.

Of the presumed-to-exist inside wall of the pyramid, he could see no evidence. He stood in a brightly lit corridor, seemingly kilometers between him and the ceiling. His doppler radar, not his strongest sense, couldn't reach quite as far as the roof, although he got some tantalizing echoes from it.

The area he occupied was a longish rectangle, five meters by perhaps fifty. Behind him was a semitransparent wall through which he could see what appeared to be a vast circular drum, several stories high, much like a fuel storage tank, yet made of the same plastic-appearing material as everything else here. In front of him, a smaller circular subchamber filled the corridor from wall to wall, yet he could see beyond it with several of his senses, knew it divided his chamber precisely in half.

To the right and left were similar, exactly parallel corridors, "visible" through walls much as the one behind him, and identical to the corridor he occupied except that they lacked the smaller circular "storage tank."

He turned left.

As far as he went along the wall, there was no exit. The available space grew smaller and narrower as he approached the circularity. Finally, he stopped, retraced his steps, and took the right-hand direction. This time, near the angle of the wall and the tank, he found a permeable area. He stepped through into the next corridor. The predominating light was blue, as it had been in the chamber he had left, but here it was slightly brighter. He crossed the corridor, found another "soft" spot in the wall, went through into a third chamber, identical to the second.

The fourth chamber was shaped differently—five-sided, but not regularly so. The only permeability was in the far right-hand wall, a very short one, forcing him to take a right turn. The next chamber was the mirror image of the last, then a series of rectangular chambers began again.

He kept walking, lonely, and, for the first time in his life, really afraid.

Seven hours, sixteen minutes, forty-four seconds.

From the inside, the pyramid was transparent.

That was the first thing Lando noticed. Outside, he could see the sun shining, the reddish color of the sand, a few scrappy shrubs, and, comfortingly close (although farther away than he would have liked) the *Millennium Falcon* sat patiently awaiting his return.

He hoped she wouldn't have to wait very long.

It was difficult to judge the thickness of the wall. It was not quite perfectly transparent, but shaded a very pale bluish tint. Behind him was an empty chamber—and he realized that there was a good chance his eyes were being tricked somehow. Not a hundred meters away, he could see one of the farther walls of the five-sided building, more sandy desert beyond. The walls came to a point perhaps two hundred meters overhead.

The trouble with all that was that the building was several kilometers in any dimension you chose to measure.

The walls, then, were sophisticated viewing devices, conveying the illusion that the building was much smaller—human-scaled, in fact—than it really was.

He called out: *"Vuffi Raa! Where are you? Mohs? Answer me!"*

There wasn't even a decent echo. He—

What was *that*? Embedded in the wall he'd come through, stuck like a fly in amber, was the Key. He reached for it—and barked his fingers badly. The wall could have been made of solid glass, and the Key was at least a meter beyond his reach. It had been his way—and Vuffi Raa's, apparently, and Mohs'—inside the pyramid.

He looked around the featureless chamber he occupied. From wall to wall, a smooth reflective floor stretched, devoid of furniture or fixtures. It was rather like being in a large, deserted warehouse. Through the walls, the sky was a slightly more brilliant blue than it had really been.

The desert was a trifle darker: red and blue make purple. The transparency had another odd effect, it made everything outside seem very far away, subtly shrunken by perspective and refraction. Perhaps the walls were curved minutely. The *Falcon* almost looked like a model, a child's toy.

Perhaps he'd better find another way out.

There had better be another way out.

Grown considerably more desperate, Vuffi Raa stopped to rest.

He was internally powered; a microfusion pile that was practically inexhaustible burned within him at all times, requiring only a minimal amount of mass to keep itself (and Vuffi Raa) going.

But the little droid was tired.

In a lifetime vastly longer than his current master would have found comfortable to contemplate, the robot could not recall ever feeling lonelier or more isolated. There, in that endless series of empty chambers, it was like being a piece in a huge meaningless game, shuffled from one spot to the next by vast, uncaring, uncommunicative fingers.

The little droid was afraid.

He'd come a considerable distance. Six featureless rectilinear rooms, after the one he'd first appeared in, with its almost transparent circular tank in the middle. Then another tankroom. The four empties, the last of which had forced him into a sharp left-hand turn. The next room had had a circularity, although there had been a narrow space to get by it. Then another empty room, another left-hand turn, three more flat blue chambers and another tank.

The pattern had repeated itself, again and again, the robot growing more disconsolate with every fruitless turn and passage. This didn't even seem like the same planet—the same reality—let alone the same building he'd somehow accidentally entered.

He wandered onward.

Thirteen hours, forty-five minutes, twenty-eight seconds had passed.

Another *right*-hand turn (the first since the initial one), two more lefts, and another right. Two more lefts. And always the same stark, empty, blue-tinted rooms, the occasional empty circular columns in their centers, more left turns, fewer rights. How long could this go on?

Nineteen hours, eleven minutes, four seconds.

Lost in thought, Mohs didn't notice that he couldn't see. It didn't matter much to him, he didn't have anyplace to go at the moment. There wasn't any hurry. He'd only been here for a minute or two, and before another minute or two went by, the Bearer and the Emissary would come and get him.

Or not.

It wasn't very important, really. He'd just realized, thinking about his loincloth once again, that if he took the long, rectangular strip of cloth, pulled it around end to end, but twisted it a half turn before joining the ends together, he'd get a very odd result: an object with only one side and one edge. How that could be, when everything had at least two sides, *had* to have, he wasn't sure. There must be some important secret to this cloth shape, he reasoned, some hint at the fundamental nature of the universe. But the secret kept eluding him, there in the dark, seemed just barely out of reach. It was annoying.

He pondered the question, picked at it, unraveled it like the homespun fabric his single garment had been made from.

It wasn't easy going, but the more he thought, the simpler things seemed to become.

Presently, they became very simple, indeed.

Mohs laughed.

Lando heard somebody laugh.

He turned, and there was Mohs—where he had not been a moment before—squatting on his heels, one arm across his naked lap, the other braced between chin and knee. Forgotten on the floor before him lay three or so meters of gray, aged loincloth, laid out in a circle, and twisted into a giant, floppy Möbius cylinder. The old man's back was toward Lando.

"Mohs!" Lando cried. "Where did you disappear to?"

The old man chuckled without turning. "Apparently the same place that you did, Captain. What time is it?"

An odd question from a naked savage, thought Lando. He glanced at his watch. "I'd say it's been perhaps twenty minutes since you vanished through the wall. What have you been doing all this time, just sitting?"

"What would you suggest I do, Captain?" The old man rose, pivoted on a heel to face Lando. "I thought it better than getting lost. You can't see your hand in front of your face in here."

"Good heavens, man! What's happened to your eyes!"

The old man blinked, lids wiped down over eyeballs that might as well have been opaque white glass.

"My eyes? There's nothing wrong with my eyes, Captain." The ancient Singer smiled. "What's wrong with yours, can't you see the darkness?"

Vuffi Raa wasn't lost, he simply didn't know where he was.

Since he'd first popped through the pyramid wall, he'd wandered through this strange, blue-lit maze for what seemed like days, taking pathways that offered no alternative. The only choice he'd had was to stay where he was or go where he could, and he'd always preferred action to inaction.

He'd taken four right turns (each carrying him through two of the oddly shaped rooms), and six left turns, not necessarily in that order. Before very long, he'd wind up exactly where he'd begun, no closer to any meaningful destination, no wiser concerning what this rat-run was intended and constructed for, and no likelier to find his friends.

Just a machine, Lando had said once. Vuffi Raa wondered if his master knew how lonely a machine could get. Vuffi Raa hadn't known, not until the last few hours. Twenty-seven of them, to be precise, plus thirty-six minutes, eleven seconds. He was three rooms past one of those with the small circular subchambers. That meant he ought to be entering a fourth, which would force him to take a left turn. After that, one more left, four more rooms, and he'd be back to where he'd started from.

And a lot more discouraged, in the bargain.

He found the soft spot in the wall, slithered through. Sure enough, none of the walls within this place—including the one he'd just passed through—would let him pass except the left-hand one. He took it, the light dimmed a little as it always did in rooms with circular tanks, and he walked automatically the length of the room, past the tank, and to the end wall.

And banged right into it. It wouldn't let him pass.

Well, here was something new. Oddly enough, it failed to hearten him, or even relieve the tedium that had become his only companion. Had he been a mammal, he'd have stood there, scratched his head, folded his arms in exasperation, and sworn.

He stood there, raised a tentacle to his chromium carapace, scratched at it absently while folding two more tentacles in disgust.

"Glitch!" he said, and meant it.

Exploring the unprecedented chamber, he traveled along the left wall, squeezed back through the narrow opening past the circular tank. The short wall through which he'd come was totally impermeable. He began feeling his way along the half of the other long wall he could reach before he had to make a circuit of the tank again—and made another discovery.

Up until now, the rounded sides of the features he chose to call tanks were just as solid and impassable as any of the other walls. This one was different. He could stick a tentacle through it. For lack of any better course, he followed the tentacle into the circular area, where, on one spot along the curved inner side, there was a deep purplish glow. As he expected, the "tank" wouldn't let him back out, so he felt the glowing section carefully. Yes, it, too was permeable.

He stepped through into a rectilinear room, exactly like the tankless blue ones he'd spent the last day wandering through.

Only these were a brilliant scarlet color.

One, two, three, four. He should be between two of the blue tankrooms, now, but there wasn't any tank in here. Five, six, seven—something odd. The far wall seemed to tug at him, and the red glow was a little fainter here. He backed up and thought.

Thirty-two hours, fifteen minutes, forty-two seconds had passed since he'd gotten into this mess. He didn't much care, now, how he got out of it.

He let the wall pull him toward itself and stepped through . . .

Lando sat by the transparent pyramid wall, his head in his hands. The last half hour had had its shocks, but this was the worst of all. Where the old Singer's eyes had been, there were now a pair of deep ugly wounds—healing rapidly, it was true, and showing no signs of infection, just as the old man showed no signs of pain. But he was blind, horribly, hideously blind.

And happy about it.

"Captain," said Mohs, "please do not be distressed. There

is nothing free in this life. I seem to have exchanged my eyes for a certain understanding. I now know what I was: a retarded savage who could see, but did not know what it was he saw. Now I am an intelligent, civilized man, who happens to be blind. Do you not think it a fair trade?"

Lando grunted, poked a finger idly at a tiny line of dust gathered in the corner between wall and floor. Something tiny sparkled there, like a speck of metal, a fleck of mirror silvering. Curious, Lando brushed the dust away from it. It was better than answering Mohs, either truthfully or insincerely. *Nothing* could make up for blindness.

"Further, Captain. My new-found reasoning capacities seem to serve me in the stead of eyes to some extent. I can tell that you are sitting to my left, turned mostly to the wall, poking with a finger in the corner. I believe I know this by deducing from the sounds you make, what I know of your personality and habits—it's quite as if I could see you."

"I'm happy for you, Mohs," Lando mumbled irritably. Suddenly, the minute sparkly bit grew larger, and Lando drew his hand back abruptly. "Son of a—look at this!"

Not noticing what he'd said to a blind man, Lando watched the corner. There was a spider there, a tiny one, very shiny, very fast. It skittered about frantically, trying to escape Lando. It couldn't have been much more than three millimeters in diameter.

Lando reached down, unafraid, let the spider race up his thumb, turned the thumb down into the palm of his other hand . . .

And watched a nearly microscopic Vuffi Raa, accelerated to sixty times normal speed, trip over his lifeline and go sprawling.

FIFTEEN

NO ONE HAD EVER ACCUSED VUFFI RAA OF BEING STUPID.

Of course he'd recognized the hundred-meter giant looming over him, the instant he'd popped out of the final red-lit chamber and through the inside wall of the pyramid. It was his master, and what surprised him was the feeling that, whatever their current predicament, he was home.

Apparently, Lando grasped the weird situation, too. He'd held his thumb down on the floor in front of Vuffi Raa, keeping it amazingly still for the full minute the little—*very* little—droid required to climb its length.

For his part, Vuffi Raa was very careful: the thumbnail at this scale was rough and full of convenient handholds, but the flesh seemed soft and spongy. He went gently, using all five tentacles and spreading them, outward and flat, to distribute his mass. One misstep would cruelly pierce his master's flesh like a needle and, perhaps, precipitate the robot into disaster.

Not that that wasn't the situation now.

With incredible slow steadiness, Lando had raised the robot up to his eye level, then across his mountainous chest, over to the other hand. Vuffi Raa tumbled down into the waiting palm, righted himself, and looked up into the giant eye that peered down at him.

"Master! What a mess! What are we going to do?"

"EEEVVVUUUFFFEEE EEEUUURRRAAAHHH," responded Lando, taking at least twenty seconds to do it, his voice low and thunderous. A human being in Vuffi Raa's position might not have been able to hear what Lando said— the little droid's range of hearing was impressive—but he'd certainly have *felt* it.

Now the robot understood his master's unnatural rock-steadiness. There seemed to be some difference in their perception of time, correlative to the difference in their sizes. Lando was living at a vastly slower rate than Vuffi Raa. He considered the problem for what would have seemed a millisecond to his master, then gave forth a series of loud chirps, spaced evenly over about a minute's time, each burst carefully shaped and calculated to blur with the ones before and after into something the giant could follow:

"Can't understand you, Master," Lando heard a tiny voice say, *"Can you hear me?"*

Lando wasn't stupid, either. He could see how quickly, jerkily, Vuffi Raa was moving about in his hand, and figured out that time—or at least metabolism—was flowing differently for each of them. He even had a good idea how Vuffi Raa was managing to communicate with him, although none whatsoever as to how he could communicate back.

He decided on short words: "Yes."

Vuffi Raa received this as "EEEYYYEEEAAASSSSS," but the part of him that was a high-powered computer quickly squashed it all together (as it had eventually learned to do when Lando called him by name) and formulated a brief reply—although it would take a much longer time to transmit:

"Ask Mohs about this."

"OOOGGGAAAIIIEEE!"

Giant-to-giant: "I say, Mohs old fellow, what does your new-found cogitational capacity tell you about *this* distressing turn of events? I believe I've got the galaxy's smallest droid here, but I don't think he's appreciating the distinction very much."

Wrapping the loincloth back around his middle by feel, the old shaman shuffled up beside the gambler, cocked an ear over the tiny robot in lieu of peering down at him with ruined eyes, and thought his answer over for a moment.

"I do not know of any Song which speaks of such a thing as this. He can hear us, can he not?"

"Yes," came the small, clear reply, almost as quickly as Mohs had asked the question, and long before Lando could respond. This method of communication seemed to work satisfactorily for the organic giants, Lando realized, but it must be agonizing unto tears for the tiny speeded-up droid, each word requiring many seconds to assemble, then the even more annoying molasses-like wait for the humans, with their slower reaction time, to answer.

"Captain," the old man said, seemingly unwilling to address a spider-sized machine directly, "I can see—in a manner of speaking—no intelligent alternative but to go on with our search for the Harp. We can do nothing for your friend here. Perhaps some solution lies ahead of us."

"Agreed," Vuffi Raa said before Lando had a chance to think about it. Meanwhile, the miniature automaton had also had time to become thoroughly fascinated with the examination of his giant master's hand. The epidermis was shingled like a shale field, and the fine ridges were like furrows made by a plow. Lando's pulse was a quiet, steady earth-

quake every few minutes. Open pores lay scattered about like gopher holes.

Finally, long after Vuffi Raa had tired of his explorations:

"AAAIII EEEGGGIIIEEESSS EEEIIIYYYOOOUUU-RRR EEERRRAAAIIITTT."

Eventually, Vuffi Raa managed to convey a question about travel arrangements. He was willing to make his exploration of the building on foot, as the humans intended to do, but his own far greater rate of operation would be more than offset by his size and the (to him) roughness of the terrain. Accordingly, he suggested that he ride, somehow, and asked diffidently how and where.

"I've always rather fancied an earring," Lando told the surprised robot. "D'you think you could manage it without tearing off my earlobe?" That would make communications a bit easier, and there would be little chance of Vuffi Raa's getting injured or dropped, since Lando would be inclined to be careful about injuring his own head.

"Captain," Mohs asked, once that had been settled, "there is supposed to be a way out of this chamber, somewhere near the center. Can you see it?"

For the relatively short time they'd been there, Lando's attention had been directed outward, through the transparent walls. Then it had all gone to Mohs and the pitiable condition of his eyes, and finally to Vuffi Raa. Now he took a good hard look around. It wasn't easy: the floor was glossy, as if it were transparent glass over some darker base. He guided the old Singer toward the center of the room, approximately fifty meters away, the little droid clinging with all five tentacles to his ear.

Before them lay a downward-slanting ramp set neatly into the floor, flush, without guardrails or other embellishment. Lando thought they hadn't noticed it before because of this, and the fact they'd been looking straight across its foreshortened length to the reflective surface on the other side.

It was strangely dim in the middle of the room, beneath the pyramid's peak. The brightly shining sun outside lent an eerie contrast, which got on Lando's nerves.

"Well, friends, shall we?" Lando asked no one in particular.

No one replied.

He shrugged, took a step—remembering, once it was too late, that this sort of thing was what had gotten him into ... well, this sort of thing in the first place. As soon as it rested on the gently downward-slanting surface, his foot began to slide forward of its own accord. He gave a hop, his other foot joined the first, and he found himself moving without walking—just as Mohs' prophetic Song had had it—on a sort of glassy, featureless elevator.

He looked behind him. Mohs was in the rear, expression a bit unsettled—apparently not very happy to realize his Songs had come true.

Well, Lando thought, are any of us ever, really?

The place that they had entered was broad, perhaps ten meters wide, and as they settled down through the floor and the tunnel seemed to level off, they saw that the roof overhead was about the same distance—ten meters—from the moving floor. The walls went straight up, tipped over into an arch overhead.

At first the walls were featureless, the same impression as above of transparency over darkness. The floor showed no signs of mechanical moving parts; an object placed upon it simply flowed along at the same rate Lando, Mohs, and Vuffi Raa were traveling. Whether the floor itself traveled with them, they were unable to determine.

"EEEIIIUUU OOOGGGAAAIII, EEEVVVUUUHHH-VVVIII EEERRRAAAHHH?"

Vuffi Raa clung to Lando's ear, watching, measuring, trying to do his part—since someone else was carrying his miniscule weight. Yet most of his mind was on the matter of his size. Assuming it was he who had diminished—never mind how or that the disparity was supposed to violate several laws of physics—he certainly didn't want to spend the rest of his life that way. Droids live a long, long time.

On the other tentacle, suppose Lando and their native companion had somehow *grown*, violating different laws. Vuffi Raa didn't think he'd have to ask them how they'd feel about that.

His contemplations were interrupted by the part of him that was watching. He gave an internal, mechanical sigh as he prepared himself for another of the tedious attempts at communication:

"Master, the corridor's beginning to curve."

"Not so loud, Vuffi Raa! Curve?" Lando glanced around. He couldn't see it; it must be very gradual. A thought occurred to him: "What's the rate? At some point, it's got to bend back on itself, and we should see the junction—for whatever good *that* does us."

"I don't think so.... It never fully leveled out.... Starting a gradual downward spiral."

"So? At what rate?" Lando repeated. The old Toka Singer listened to this exchange as it went on, a strange look on his blinded face. "What's the apparent diameter of the spiral?"

"Whose scale?"

Lando chuckled. "A good question. Make it mine, if you don't mind. I've got to figure it out, haven't I?"

Vuffi Raa refrained from saying that Lando hadn't been much good so far at figuring out anything—and only partly because communications were such a chore. Instead, he simply divided everything his sensors told him by approximately sixty.

"Ten klicks at current rate. Drops a hundred meters every thirty kilometers."

"Can you tell how fast this thing is carrying us?"

"About twenty kph. One full spiral every one-twenty-third of a planetary revolution."

* * *

The journey went on and on. Hours passed.

It was Vuffi Raa who first noticed the changes in the walls.

"Master. Please observe that something is visible."

"I see it." Lando peered through the transparency. Where before there had been inky blackness, now some form and structure could be seen, like a highway cut through a mountain pass. "We're out of the pyramid! Below it!"

SIXTEEN

THEY TRAVELED THROUGH THE HEART OF THE PLANET.

This was not precisely true, as Vuffi Raa was already pointing out, but it was a metaphor that suited Lando.

The geological strata they were seeing dated, according to the little droid, from the beginnings of life on Rafa V. Beds of stone formed by tiny microscopic creatures living in seas that no longer existed on the ancient, dried-up sphere alternated with slabs of solidified lava from volcanic eruptions. Vuffi Raa's fine vision—and perhaps the fact that he was so small—enabled him to see and describe the smallest details through the transparent glass.

"And here we see . . . Master . . . the evidence of the first cellular colonies . . . the precursors of multicelled animals."

"Don't call me Master, especially when you're lecturing me. Do you want a bite of this, Mohs?"

Lando had delved into the pockets of his survival parka for water and condensed rations. Vuffi Raa hadn't any need of them, but the old man surprised Lando by accepting only a small portion from the plastic canteen.

Otherwise, the ancient High Singer had been strangely quiet for hours, watching the walls, peering ahead into a gloom that was something other than darkness, listening to Vuffi Raa. How much the old man understood of the droid's paleontological dissertations, he had no way of guessing.

"But if we're seeing the slow, steady progress of microscopic life," Lando asked Vuffi Raa, "doesn't that mean we must be gaining altitude again?"

"On the contrary...Master...the corridor leveled out some time ago...and straightened.... We're traveling in a diagonal upthrust formation."

For some reason, this bothered Lando. He wished the robot had kept him informed on the shape and direction of their travel. More, this was almost as if...as if...

"They chose this route deliberately, didn't they? So we'd see what we're seeing!"

"They, Captain?" Mohs spoke up, surprising Lando. The old man had long since discovered that he could travel on a moving sidewalk just as easily by sitting down as standing. Lando had joined him, and they were sitting a few feet apart now. Lando had been thinking about taking a nap before the walls grew transparent and the geology lectures began. He was still thinking about it.

"You know perfectly well who I mean. There's some purpose to all this, isn't there?"

"If so, Captain, the Songs do not—"

"I'll bet they don't! Mohs, the primary purpose of those Songs of yours was to make sure somebody, someday, wound up sitting precisely where you are."

"So I, too, had surmised."

Lando searched through his pockets, found a cigarette. He didn't smoke much at all, and when he did, he preferred cigars. Whoever had packed this parka—an Imperial surplus model—had left very little missing. Lando lit a dried-up cigarette with a tiny electric coil built into one sleeve of the jacket.

"The question, then, is *why*. What's so flaming important about your seeing all these rocks and suchlike?"

The old man lifted his sightless head. "There must be a better word than 'seeing,' Captain."

"Great Heavens, man, I'd almost—, He *had* almost forgotten about Mohs' eyes. At least the hideous wounds were healing.

Yet Mohs had not been moving like a newly blinded man, had not been stumbling and groping. He had peered at the walls, down the tunnel, listened to Vuffi Raa as if he could—

"What do you mean, 'a *better* word,' Mohs? Is there some sense better than seeing?"

The Toka Singer swiveled himself where he sat on the floor and faced Lando. He drew in a deep breath, then let it out.

"It would appear so, Captain. You are carrying the Emissary on your right ear. You have a container of water in your left hand, the remains of a food-stick in your right. Your coat is unfastened; the shirt beneath has a missing fastener, second from the top. You hold a burning weed-stick in the same hand which holds the canteen. It is approximately one-third consumed."

Lando was as impressed as he ever was by anything. "What color are my eyes?"

"They are the color of deceit, the color of avarice, the color of—"

"Enough, enough! Don't go getting poetic on us. Somehow you are 'seeing' all these things. Any idea how: clairvoyance, telepathy, psychometry . . ."

"I do not know the meaning of these words, Captain. I can hear the water gurgling, the weed-stick crackling, the tones within your voice and that of the Emissary. I smell things and feel vibrations in the floor. Here it is warm, there it is cold. Pictures form themselves in my mind. My remaining senses assemble information which tells me everything my eyes once did."

"Pretty good trick. How many fingers am I—*ow*! Take it easy, Vuffi Raa, that's my earlobe you're destroying!"

"Apologies... Master.... Observe the walls.... There are the first large creatures to appear on this world."

Vuffi Raa's method of communication was far from perfect, but it didn't fail to convey his excitement. Lando wondered what was so terrific about the fossils of old marine animals. Why, they looked like ordinary urchins, starfish, and the like. Perhaps that was what had moved the little robot. These things weren't unlike him in their rough anatomy: five-sided, five-limbed.

That didn't account for Mohs' excitement: "Behold! Look upon the very ancestors of Those whose name it is not wise to speak in this place!"

"You mean the Sharu?" Lando said defiantly. He hated mumbo jumbo, even in a good cause, and this wasn't.

"Yes, Captain," the old man resignedly sighed, "I mean the Sharu."

They were nothing more than a bunch of formerly slimy starfish, no matter *whose* ancestors they were.

The hours wore on, Vuffi Raa and Mohs alternating in rapture over what they observed embedded in the walls. Lando yawned, slid over onto the moving floor surface, arranged the hood of his parka comfortably, and did a little sliding of his own, in the direction of sleep.

The floor was solid, but resilient, and it was warm.

Even in his sleep, the science lectures wouldn't leave him alone. He recapitulated the slow, steady progress—boring every step of the way—from the tiny, disgusting single-celled inhabitants of the planet's soupy primeval waters, through the first colony organisms, up into multicelled animals, and from there to things with backbones and legs which eventually crawled out on the land.

Oddly, the further these imaginary entities got, climbing

the tree of evolution, the vaguer and more nebulous they grew in Lando's mind. Queer, shadowy shapes beat at one another with broken tree limbs. Even more intangible figures took those tree limbs, scratched the dirt with them, and planted the first seeds. By the time the ancestors of the Sharu were building tiny, crude cities, it was almost as if the cities built themselves and were inhabited by invisible citizens.

Continents were explored, migrations carried out. Wars were won and lost, with rapidly increasing technology. Discoveries were made, more wars fought. The pre-Sharu touched the boundaries of space in primitive explosive-powered machines, depositing the first installment of the junk the *Millennium Falcon* had had to fly through, getting to Rafa V.

All the while, Lando experienced a growing sense of unease, some vague pain or nagging that made his sleep less restful than it might have been. He'd had no idea, all day, where they were going. There wasn't any choice in the matter for him: he had to find the Mindharp, and then figure out how to get out of the tunnel, away from the ruins, off the stinking planet, and, ultimately, clear of the Rafa once and for all.

They'd never catch *him* bringing mynocks into the Rafa System again!

Or anything else.

The sense of unease grew, gradually metamorphosing into something resembling real pain. Lando tossed and turned in his sleep, but kept on dreaming.

The ancestors of the Sharu had built roads and buildings that wouldn't be unfamiliar to any civilized inhabitant of the galaxy. They had traveled in powered vehicles, eventually spread themselves to other planets of the system. At first they endured the harsh conditions on some of these globes, living in domes or underground. Finally, they had begun transforming them into replicas of their own home planet.

It hadn't always been a desert. There had been oceans and trees and lakes and snow-covered mountains. There had been moisture in the air, and weather. How long ago all that had been, the part of Lando that did the dreaming wasn't prepared to guess. How long does it take for the seas to go away?

Gradually, however, as their technology surpassed that which was currently available in Lando's civilization, the shapes of buildings changed, the roads disappeared. The unseen entities who were becoming the Sharu fought no more wars, but struggled, instead, with the environment. No rock, whirling in its independent orbit around the Rafa sun, was too insignificant to be altered into a garden. To what precise purpose became increasingly unclear. Cities ceased to resemble anything that made sense. The first of the gigantic plastic structures appeared—on Rafa V. Then they appeared on the other planets, as well.

Taken altogether, they were nightmarish things. Lando squirmed in his sleep, flailed his arms and sweated. Every surface and angle was somehow *wrong*, things were added that seemed without function, passageways tapered out into tiny pipelines, hair-fine fractures became vast thorough-fares, in no logical order. The seas began to vanish, red sand replacing landscape everywhere. Had something gone wrong with the Sharu environment, or did they like it better the new way, plan it?

Lando sank deeper into a dreamless, pain-filled sleep. His last thought was a question: would this passage funnel down until the inexorably moving floor ground them into tiny pieces?

Lando woke up.

Somewhere, for a fraction of a second, he had the feeling that everything made sense after all. Then the feeling went away and left him with a terrible lingering headache.

"Vuffi Raa, are you awake? You're going to have to find another perch for a while, my whole head hurts!" He rolled over on his back from the curled-up position he'd taken in the night.

"Masteryou'reawakeatlasthowdoyoufeel?"

He sat up—a sudden blast of pain hit him and he settled back again for a moment. "Take it a little slower, will you?" He lifted a hand to his ear. "Hop down a minute while I get rid of this headache."

He felt a feather touch his palm. The pain subsided. Bringing his hand down, he looked at Vuffi Raa. Something was funny, but he couldn't place it in his present groggy state.

The walls rolled by, this time showing discarded metal and plastic containers, parts of machinery and electronics frozen into the geological matrix. How long does a civilization have to last before its radios and televisions become fossils?

"Now, what was it you were saying, little fellow?"

"Merely . . . greeted . . . you . . . Asked . . . how . . . you . . . feel."

"Lousy, but thanks for asking. Anything interesting happen in the night?" He scrounged around for a cigarette, started thinking about which of the ration bars to eat for breakfast.

"It . . . is . . . nighttime . . . now . . . outside. . . . Master . . . You . . . slept . . . through . . . the . . . day."

"I don't see that it makes all that much difference, down here. Where's Mohs?" Lando had glanced around, up and down the tunnel, and hadn't seen the old man. Perhaps he'd—

"What . . . Master?"

"We seem to be having some difficulty understanding one another this—er, afternoon. I said, where's Mohs, did he wander off somewhere?"

"Master . . . there is something I must tell you."

Lando felt a vague alarm. "What's that, old watch-movement?"

"I believe . . . from measurements . . . that you're shrinking."

"What?"

"Everything is shrinking. . . . The tunnel grows narrower by the kilometer. . . . You have shrunk just enough that my weight upon you causes pain. . . . The previous rate at which I communicated is too fast. . . . We are nearing each other's size and time-passage."

"Which could mean just as well that you're growing, did you ever think of that?" Lando examined the tiny robot in his hand. Let's see, he'd estimated Vuffi Raa's previous size at perhaps three millimeters. Yes, no question of it, he was very nearly twice that size now and his miniscule weight was actually perceptible in Lando's hand.

"Yes. . . . I considered it. . . . I think you are shrinking."

"Well, I think you're growing. What about Mohs?"

"Who . . . Master. . . . Who is Mohs?"

"Vuffi Raa, don't do this to me! Mohs—the High Singer of the Toka—the old guy who *led* us here! *Mohs!*"

There was a long, long pause. It must have been vastly longer to the speeded-up droid. Finally:

"Master . . . I recall no Mohs. . . . Are you certain you feel all right?"

SEVENTEEN

As the tunnel carried them along, they argued.

"Who was it that we met in the bar, who sang the Songs that pointed the way to Rafa IV?"

"Why, Master, something that Rokur Gepta said must have given you the clue, and you guessed. Very good guessing, Master, highly commendable."

"Well, then, damnit, what about that crowd at the port. Who had been leading the singing?"

"Why, no one, Master, it was simply community chanting, spontaneous on the part of the natives."

"Arghhh! Okay, why did we land at the pyramid—never mind, I know: it was the biggest building on the planet. Tell me this: if there wasn't any Mohs, who ambushed us, shot you full of holes, and carried me off to the life-orchard to die?"

"The natives, of course, Master. But there wasn't any chief or head witch doctor or whatever. The Toka don't have enough social structure for that."

"Or to build crossbows? Look, Vuffi Raa, I *couldn't* have made up that part about eating a lizard, I just *couldn't*."

"What do you expect me to say, Master?"

"I expect you to say that this is all an elaborate practical joke, and that you're sorry and will be a good little droid from now on." Lando shook the plastic package. There weren't any cigarettes left. "Life is just full of annoyances these days."

Vuffi Raa stood on the floor by Lando's knee. He was five or six centimeters tall, by then, looking very much like one of those tropical spiders that eat birds.

"I wish I could do that," he squeaked, no longer coding his messages in pulses. He had to make a conscious effort to slow them down for his still-gigantic master. "What reason would I have to lie, Master?"

Lando crushed the pack, started to throw it away, then, looking around him at the clean, uncluttered tunnel, thought better of it and put it in his pocket. "I'm not saying you're lying, Vuffi Raa. One of us is wrong, that's all. By the Eternal Core, I can describe the old man to you in the finest detail, from the tattoo on his wrinkled forehead to the dirt on his wrinkled feet!"

Vuffi Raa said nothing to that. He simply sat there growing—or watching his master shrink. That was something else they hadn't been able to agree about, but they'd tired of arguing about it.

They were also tired of asking one another when the journey would be over. Lando extracted the deck of *sabacc* cards he carried with him, began to shuffle them. Vuffi Raa looked on with interest.

"Did you know, old pentapod, that these things were once used for telling fortunes?" He shuffled the deck again, cut it, and began laying the cards out on the floor.

"Highly irrational and unscientific, Master."

"Don't call me Master. I know what you mean, though— except that sometimes they can help you solve a problem, simply by getting you to look at it in a way you hadn't thought to before."

"I've heard that said, Master, but so can a sudden blow to the head, if you're looking for random stimuli."

That's right, Lando thought, what I really need now is a fresh machine to banter with. The first card to fall was the Commander of Staves, one which Lando had often associated with himself. It was the apparently chance appearance of the right card—as happened so often—that made him wonder if his "scientific" analysis was all there was to the things.

"That's me," he explained to the robot, "a messenger on a fool's errand. Let's see what stands in the way." He dealt a second card, laid it across the first. "Great Gadfry!" he exclaimed.

"What is it, Master?"

"Not what, *who*. It's Himself—the Evil One. I'd guess that to be Rokur Gepta. Hold on, now, it's changing."

As *sabacc* card-chips are prone to do now and again, the second card transformed itself into the Legate of Coins— but the image was upside-down.

"Duttes Mer!" laughed Lando. "A being corrupt and evil if ever there was one! Well, that makes sense, even though it tells us nothing new. Let's see what else."

The third card he placed above the others. The Five of Sabres, Lando explained, represented his own conscious motivations, in this case, the desire to relieve the weak and unwary of the burden of their excess cash. He chuckled, dealt a card below the others, indicating his deeper, possibly subconscious motives. He groaned.

"The Legate of Staves. Don't tell me I'm a do-gooder at heart!"

"Master, this is simply a random distribution of images, don't take it seriously."

Lando looked at the little robot cautiously. "I think I've just been insulted. Well, the next card should tell us something. It represents the past, things coming to an end."

It was the Six of Sabres. Lando placed it to the left.

"Oh-ho! This usually denotes a journey, but its position indicates the journey is nearly at an end. What do you think of that?"

"I think, Master, that journeys can end in many ways, not all of them pleasant or productive."

"That's what I keep you around for, to bring me down whenever I feel too good, to remind me that every silver lining has a cloud. Say, you know, you're getting bigger—eight, maybe nine centimeters. And your voice is changing, too."

The little robot didn't reply, but simply watched Lando lay the next card down to the right of the center pair.

"Flame and famine! You spoiled the run, Vuffi Raa—it's the Destroyed Starship!"

"Does that mean harm will come to the *Falcon*, Master?"

"Don't call me Master. I thought you didn't believe in any of this."

"I don't. But what does it mean?"

"Cataclysmic changes in the near future, death and destruction. It may be the worst card in the whole deck. Maybe. One thing I've learned from all this: there's always a worse card. This next will tell us what will happen to us and how we'll react to it."

"*We*, Master?"

"There you go again—*great*: the Satellite. It means a lot of fairly nasty things, things that you find under rocks. Mostly it means deception, deceit, betrayal." He looked closely at the robot again. "Are you getting ready to double-cross me, my mechanical minion?"

"There, Master, is the greatest danger in such mystical pursuits. You trusted me before you started playing with those card-chips, didn't you?"

"I still do, Vuffi Raa. The next card, up above the Satellite, here, is supposed to tell us where we'll find ourselves next. Hmmm. I wonder what that means?"

The Wheel sat shimmering on the card-chip, an image denoting luck, both good and bad, the beginning and the ending of things, random chance, final outcome—it gave Lando no information whatsoever.

The third card in that part of the array, placed in line above the Satellite and the Wheel, represented future obstacles. Lando cringed when he saw what had appeared.

"Gepta again! Well, I suppose that's only logical. Want to see the final outcome, old clockwork? Well, you're going to, anyway. Here we go. Well, that's not too bad, after all. It's the Universe. It means we'll have a shot at everything we want to do. Join the human race and see the world. Something like that."

"Master."

"Yes, Vuffi Raa, what is it?"

"Master, that Six of Sabres: that's a journey over with?"

"That's what I said although it can mean other things, in other—"

"Master, our journey's over with."

And, indeed, so it appeared to be. The floor slowed as they came upon the towering doorway of a chamber large enough to park a fleet of spaceships in. A long, long distance away, something resembling a giant altar was raised, all the lights in the cavernous room focused upon it.

Even from several hundred meters off, Lando could tell it was the Mindharp of Sharu. It hurt his eyes to look at it.

EIGHTEEN

It wasn't as easy as all that.

There were other things inside the hall besides the podium or altar where the Mindharp stood, and a giant replica of the Key Lando had carried until the wall of the pyramid had taken it.

"What do you make of that, Vuffi Raa?"

The robot, standing now as high as Lando's knee, peered into the same odd well-lighted gloom that had filled the tunnel behind them. The light was a brownish amber and seemed to emanate from the floor. The room, a vast auditorium of a place, was lined with something between sculpture and painting—a pageant that seemed, to the gambler, to recapitulate his dreams of the night before.

Here, at the entrance, shaggy forms, barely erect, shambled along the walls in a frozen march, growing straighter, taller, beginning to carry things in their hands, to lose their furry coverings, to wear clothing.

Lando and Vuffi Raa followed the right wall, which curved gently into the vast circularity that was the chamber of the Mindharp. By the time the figures on the wall were playing with internal combustion engines and rocketry, the pair had only walked a few dozen meters. Uncounted thousands of centuries of history lay ahead of them.

The robot hadn't spoken. Lando looked down at him. His eye was glowing peculiarly—or perhaps the peculiarity was in the lighting of the chamber.

"Vuffi Raa, did you hear me?"

"Why yes, Lando," the droid said, seeming to be waking from a sort of walking dream. "What do I make of this? The same that you do—that this is somehow the center of Sharu culture. What they left behind of it, anyway. That the Harp is somehow even more important than we thought it was."

Lando hadn't been thinking that at all. He'd been thinking that the chamber was a place of worship, that the figures on the wall were human—Toka—that the bas-relief murals would convey to them the story of how they arose on some far-off planet and came to the Rafa System. That somewhere along the wall the story would be told of how they met the Sharu and discovered their masters.

He didn't want to wait. "I'm going on across the room— enough of this historical nonsense. Coming with me?"

Vuffi Raa turned, followed Lando without a word.

It was a long, long trip. The Sharu had discovered the same secret that many human cultures had: that if you make the floors of a public building slick enough, keep them polished and slippery, they'll force the people who have to walk there into little mincing steps that magnify the distances and humble the spirit—just as high ceilings tend to do.

Lando wasn't having any. He took a few running steps and slid along the floor.

"Wheee! This is fun! Come on, old tinhorn, try it!"

"Master!" said the robot in a scandalized voice. "Have you no respect?"

Lando stopped, gave the robot a sober look. "Not a grain of it—not when it's being imposed on me by the architecture."

He took another running start, slid several meters this time. The robot had to hurry to catch up. By the time he had, he was very nearly his original height.

"Lando," he said, "speaking of architecture, there's something very odd about this place."

Lando had to stop to catch his breath. He sat down on the floor.

"That would be consistent with everything else around here. What is it this time?"

"Well, from the entrance, the room looked circular, with a high domed ceiling, and perhaps a thousand meters across the floor to the altar."

Lando looked around. "Still seems that way to me."

"And to my vision, too. But, checking with radar and a number of extra senses, the room is ovoid—shaped like an egg with a big end and a small end. The big end was the entrance. The roof keeps getting closer to the floor."

Lando had another flash of his dreams. Something Vuffi Raa said earlier had triggered the first, something about the idea that it wasn't he, the robot who was growing, but Lando who was shrinking. Yet if that were true—the tunnel had seemed to stay the same size the duration of the two-day trip—then the moving passageway had to have been shrinking. Lando had appeared to Vuffi Raa to be a hundred and ten or twenty meters tall in the beginning. Now he was back to being a little shy of two. The corridors had to have been shrinking accordingly.

At that rate, when they reached the Mindharp, Vuffi Raa would tower over Lando, and they'd both have to travel on hands and knees to reach the artifact.

"HALT!" said a voice.

"What?" Vuffi Raa and Lando cried simultaneously.

"IT IS NOT PERMITTED TO CROSS THE HALL."

"What happens if we do?" inquired Lando.

The voice paused, seemed confused. "WELL, I'M NOT SURE I KNOW. NO ONE EVER ASKED ME. BUT IT IS NOT PERMITTED."

Lando opened his mouth—

"Just who in the Hall are you, anyway?" Vuffi Raa said. Lando looked at the robot sharply. He hated having his good lines stolen. It was exactly what he'd been planning to say, himself.

"WHY, I AM THE HALL, OF COURSE. YOU'RE SUPPOSED TO LOOK AT THE EXHIBIT AS YOU APPROACH THE SACRED OBJECT."

"And it's your job," Lando suggested, "to make sure we do? Well, let's get a few things straight here, Hall: I've been tugged along by everything that's happened so far. I'm not going to let an empty room tell me what to do. Now answer me truthfully: does anything bad or dangerous happen to someone if they *don't* skulk along the wall like vermin?"

"NO, I DON'T SUPPOSE IT DOES."

"Then I guess we'll go on. You don't happen to have a cigarette, do you?"

"I'M AFRAID I DON'T KNOW WHAT YOU MEAN."

"I thought you were going to say that. Come on, Vuffi Raa."

They continued across the broad expanse of the Hall, Lando sliding occasionally just to demonstrate his spirit. Vuffi Raa's legs twinkled in the weird lighting. Lando had a thought:

"Hey, Hall?"

"YES, HAVE YOU DECIDED TO GO BACK TO THE WALL?"

"No. I was just wondering: how much do you know about this place?"

"ABOUT MYSELF?"

"No, about the pyramid and the moving tunnel we were in before we got here."

The Hall considered. "A GREAT DEAL. WHAT, SPECIFICALLY WOULD YOU LIKE TO KNOW?"

"Well, just to begin, what size am I?"

A very long pause this time. "IN WHAT UNITS OF MEASUREMENT?"

"Skip it, then. What I really want to know is: was I gigantic a few kilometers back, or was my friend, here, very tiny?"

"DOES IT MATTER?"

"Of *course* it matters. Would I ask, otherwise?"

"Organic entities seem to take considerable delight in doing things to no good purpose," Vuffi Raa offered. "But in this case, Hall, I'd be interested in knowing, too."

"Right," Lando said under his breath, "so the two of us can compare notes on the frailties of humankind. Play your cards right, Vuffi Raa, cozy up to this Hall and they may make you a telephone booth or something."

"VERY WELL. THE CHANGES IN DIMENSION WERE WROUGHT ON THE ORGANIC LIFE-FORMS HERE. IT IS A NECESSARY PART OF THE PROCESS WHICH CULMINATES, PROPERLY, IN TRAVELING AROUND THE CIRCUMFERENCE OF THE HALL AS YOU ARE INTEN—"

"Skip the commercial, Hall," said Lando, "and get on with the explanation."

"VERY WELL. THIS INSTRUMENTALITY IS CAPABLE OF ALTERING THE PROPORTIONS OF INANIMATE MATTER AS WELL, BUT IT MUST BE IN THE PROXIMITY OF ORGANIC LIFE. OTHERWISE, IT IS ABSORBED BY THE MAINTENANCE SYSTEMS."

Vuffi Raa described his journey through the blue and red maze. "Can you tell me what all that was about?"

"CERTAINLY. YOU WERE MISTAKEN BY THE WALL FOR A SMALL HOUSEKEEPING DEVICE AND ROUTED THERE FOR REPROGRAMMING AND REPAIR. HAVE YOU BEEN REPAIRED?"

"Not that I know of."

Lando laughed. "Any secret urges to sweep up or take out the garbage?"

"Lando, this is serious. I want to know what happened!"

"Touchy! Okay, I concede, I grew, I shrank—but I've got you on another one: Mohs. The Hall said organic life-forms, plural."

"QUITE CORRECT, SIR, YOUR INTESTINAL FLORA, OTHER SYMBIOTIC ORGANISMS, ALL WERE GREATLY ALTERED IN SIZE, THEN BROUGHT BACK TO NORMAL MAGNITUDE AS PART OF—"

"What about Mohs. Was there *another* human being with us when we entered, and what happened to him?"

The hall was silent—a guilty silence if ever there was one. Lando realized suddenly that relations between mechanical intelligences weren't all that different from those between organic ones.

"Well?"

More silence.

Lando looked at Vuffi Raa. "That thing mistook you for a maintenance bug, and bummed up your memory trying to 'repair' you. *That's* why you don't remember Mohs. Now it feels ashamed."

Vuffi Raa looked at Lando. "I certainly hope so, Master, I certainly hope so. What are we going to do, once we reach the Harp?"

"Shhhh! The walls have ears. We're going to use it in whatever manner was intended—rather, take it to somebody who knows how to and let him do it."

"You mean the governor?"

"That fat ape? No, I mean Gepta. He's the one who really says when we get to leave this lousy system."

They shuffled onward, trying, occasionally, to get the hall's attention again. Since it obviously hadn't gone away, it must have been ignoring them. Finally they reached the base of the raised platform on which the Mindharp stood.

It wasn't as bad as Lando had predicted: the ceiling *was* much lower—Vuffi Raa was now his old familiar size again—and the room felt smaller, but it was still huge and awe-imposing. As was the altar.

A dozen meters high, it was cut from a single perfectly transparent slab of what appeared to be life-crystal. It was hexagonal in cross section, with corners one could practically cut himself on. Otherwise, it was smooth and featureless.

It would be a long, difficult climb.

Lando sat down to consider the problem. His survival kit included no rope, suction cups, antigravs. Its designers had anticipated he would be among others—fellow soldiers—and had shared out supplies in a package that was sold originally to an entire squad. They had not anticipated that survival would necessitate committing a burglary.

"Any ideas, Vuffi Raa?"

"No, Master. If I were small again . . ."

"You never were small, remember? We argued about that and you won."

"Oh, that's right. You argued so persuasively that I forgot for a moment."

"Vuffi Raa, I think that's the first nice thing you've ever said to me."

"You're welcome, Master."

"Don't call me Master." He thought some more, then: "Hey, Hall?"

"MAY I BE OF ASSISTANCE?"

"I hope so. How come you didn't answer us back there?"

"I'M SORRY, I WAS THINKING ABOUT SOMETHING. MAY I HELP YOU NOW?"

"Sure. Does this pylon sink into the floor or anything?"

"NO, I'M AFRAID THAT IT DOES NOT."

"You don't happen to have a ladder handy, do you?"

"NO, SIR, I AM NOT SO EQUIPPED."

Lando mused for a long time. Despite his long sleep, he

was tired and hungry—jacket rations aren't everything their manufacturers claim for them. In fact, they aren't *anything* their manufacturers claim, except that they'll keep you alive.

"Say! Can you make me big again?"

"CONGRATULATIONS, SIR, YOU HAVE PASSED THE TEST. YES, I CAN ENLARGE YOUR SIZE. DO YOU WISH ME TO BEGIN NOW?"

"Can you make me normal again, afterward? The size I am now—provided that's the size I started out before we entered the pyramid?"

"IMMEDIATELY UPON YOUR REQUEST, SIR."

He looked at Vuffi Raa. "Well, here we go again."

"'We,' Master?"

"Now don't start that! Okay, Hall, let's do it!"

This time it was perceptible. Lando watched the room and everything in it shrink around him, Vuffi Raa grow smaller, the altar shorter. It only took a few moments. "How the devil does this work, anyway, Hall? I thought it was supposed to be impossible—cube–square relationships and my bones not supporting my weight above a certain size and everything. That's why I figured Vuffi Raa had shrunk—plenty of problems there, but fewer, I think."

"OH, NO PROBLEMS AT ALL, SIR," the Hall began. Lando noticed that its voice wasn't disturbed at all by the change in scales. Good engineers, those Sharu. "WHAT ARE YOU, NO OFFENSE, SIR, BUT ORGANIZED INFORMATION? WHAT DOES IT MATTER HOW DENSELY THAT INFORMATION IS COMPRESSED? AN OLD-FASHIONED BOOK MAY BE PRINTED UPON THICK PAPER, WITH THE LINES DOUBLE-SPACED. STILL, IT IS THE SAME INFORMATION, IS IT NOT?"

"You trying to tell me I've been sort of spread-out, like? I'm not sure I like that thought. Well, here we are. Vuffi Raa? That's all right, you don't have to talk back. Just help me with this thing once I get it down—it's going to be *big*."

At present, the Mindharp rested on the flat upper surface of the pylon. It was a precise replica of the Key, except for size, and, in his present condition, it felt the same to Lando as the Key had. He reached down to take it, it came away without resistance. He started to put it in his pocket—

"Master . . . don't . . . do . . . that."

"Right! It'd mess up my jacket a bit when I shrank back down, wouldn't it? Okay, Hall, let's lower me back where I belong."

Silence.

"Hall? Hey, you're supposed to shrink me again! Get with it!"

There was no reply.

"Look, Hall, if you don't listen, I'm going to take this obscene artifact and—"

"OH, I'M VERY SORRY, SIR. WOOL-GATHERING AGAIN. I HAVE AN INCREASING TENDENCY TO THAT, AS THE MILLENNIA ROLL ON. I TAKE IT YOU WISH TO BE REDUCED AGAIN."

"You take it right."

With that, Lando began to shrink once more, the Mindharp growing perceptibly in his hands as he did so. He stooped gently, set it on the floor beside Vuffi Raa, straightened, and folded his arms over his chest.

The Mindharp was an armful when Lando had been restored to his natural size. Perhaps a meter in its greatest extent, it was even more visually distressing than the tiny model he had played with in the beginning.

"Vuffi Raa, take one end of this. Hall, how do we get out of here?"

"BEHIND THE PILLAR, SIR, AND GOOD LUCK."

"Well, good luck to you, too. Maybe someday they'll hold concerts here."

"I CERTAINLY HOPE NOT, SIR. I RATHER LIKE THE PEACE AND QUIET."

Behind the pylon was a wall.

Embedded in the wall was a Key.

Perhaps it was the same Key, Lando thought—this building seemed to like little jokes like that. The question was, how did you use it? It protruded somehow from the wall.

He let one hand go from the Mindharp, reached out to touch its smaller counterpart.

There was a flash! and a hole began opening in the wall, like the iris of an ancient camera. Lando and Vuffi Raa stepped through.

Into the busy daytime streets of Teguta Lusat.

NINETEEN

"OFFICER," VUFFI RAA DEMANDED, SUMMONING THE first constabulary cop he saw on the street. The robot pointed a tentacle at Lando. "Arrest this man immediately. Orders of the governor."

Lando stopped, stunned. They hadn't taken three steps away from the side of the Sharu ruin they'd emerged from. He looked back—the aperture they'd walked through was gone. He held the Mindharp to his chest, walked back a step, another, until his back was against the wall.

"Why, you little—"

"That'll be enough of that," the cop ordered. "I can't arrest a man on the word of a machine. I'll have to check it out with H.Q." He touched the side of his helmet, communed momentarily with the radio inside it, then waved off with one hand the small crowd that was beginning to gather.

Lando took a small, quiet step sideways. No one seemed to notice. He took another, and another. Only a few more steps to a corner where he just might be able to—

"Officer!" Vuffi Raa shouted. "He's trying to get away!"

"Thanks a lot, you atom-powered fink!"

The policeman drew his blaster, held it steady on Lando's chest. "Well—first time I've ever heard of a droid with a security clearance like that, but—hold still, you! We'll have some transportation in a minute, then we'll all take a nice little ride."

The governor's office looked much the same as it had before, even to the absence of Rokur Gepta the Sorcerer of Tund. With the Mindharp lying across the crystalline desk, Lando wondered why the wizard wasn't present to claim the prize he'd sought so avidly.

He didn't wonder very long.

"Good afternoon," Duttes Mer said, entering from the right and easing himself into his chair. "I see you have the object. Very good. You could tell me one little thing, though, if you would be so kind."

Lando was standing between two of Teguta Lusat's finest once again. This time Vuffi Raa was present, standing beside the governor's desk.

"Anything you want to know," Lando said, trying hard for cheerfulness and not quite making it.

"EXACTLY WHERE HAVE YOU BEEN THESE LAST FOUR MONTHS?" The governor calmed himself down, straightened his neckcloth, blinked.

"Four months?" Lando asked, reeling from one astonishing development after—so *that* was it! The time differential. What had seemed like a couple of days to him had actually been sixty times that long. "Governor, you wouldn't believe me if I told you. Ask your treacherous friend, here. He'll tell you—unless he's a congenital liar."

"Don't be too hard on the droid, Captain. He did what he was programmed to do: play the Emissary's part so that the natives would help you find the Harp. Also, to report to me the instant the Harp was in your possession. It would seem I've had a stroke of luck in that respect, however.

How is it that you flew to Rafa V and returned here without being picked up on planetary defense sensors? We really have a nice, modern system, you know."

"*You* tell him, Vuffi Raa, since you're such a blabbermouth anyway."

"Sir," the robot said, "the Sharu appear to have had some method of matter transport. I'm not certain when the transition occurred, and I am told that you lost track of my telemetry the instant we entered the pyramid on Rafa V. The shift could have been any time afterward, from the inside wall of the pyramid to the aperture through which we stepped into the street here in Teguta Lusat."

The governor patted his stumpy fingers together. "Well, well. A technological bonus, if we can unravel its secret. In the meantime, as I said, a stroke of unexpected luck. You see, Captain, my, er, colleague is orbiting Rafa V this very minute, waiting for your emergence there."

"Haw, haw. *I* am *here*. And *I* have the Mindharp. It would appear that I am something of a lucky gambler, too, wouldn't you say?"

Lando shrugged indifferently. This wasn't going to turn out good, no matter what he did, and there wasn't any point in giving the fat slob any satisfaction.

"Come now, Captain, consider: Rokur Gepta hired an anthropologist—a *real* one, mind you, with genuine credentials—to investigate the system. The poor fellow thought he was working for me, which gave us the opportunity to appropriate his paycheck from Imperial funds, and yielded Gepta the enjoyment of misdirection he seems to treasure so much for its own sake.

"Meanwhile, we set a little trap. In return for the offer of a new job, once his investigations here were finished, the anthropologist went to Oseon 2795 in search of, well, shall we say a suitably gullible individual to do our work for us."

Interested despite himself, and aware that Mer's desire for, what, approval? might show him a way out of the mess, Lando asked, "Why didn't you just hire yourself another sucker—or let your tame scientist get the Mindharp for you? Why me, and why maneuver me into it, rather than simply coming out and—"

The governor laughed. "You know the legends. It had to be a wandering adventurer from the stars, a stranger to the Toka, someone they hadn't seen snooping around, recording their chants and so forth. And the truth. Why, Captain, if you had known the truth about the Mindharp, *you* would be about to assume absolute power over the minds of everyone in the system, rather than myself. That is another mistake my esteemed colleague made. Thus we looked for a freighter captain down on his luck—and on Oseon 2795 everybody's down on his luck—in a place where we had the, er, cooperation of local law-enforcement personnel. We let you think you'd won the robot, and put you in a position where you had to flee—"

"Oh?" the gambler asked beneath raised eyebrows. "Well, suppose I'd fled to the Dela System, as I'd intended, or simply—"

"There was the 'treasure' as an inducement, plus the fact that you had a valuable asset to claim in the droid, here. And, of course, if you hadn't come, our *Ottdefa* Osuno Whett would simply have found a new prospect. You were our first—I'm rather proud of the *Ottdefa*."

Lando shook his head resignedly. "I get it. That's why Vuffi Raa was left here: if you'd missed your chance with me, and I'd had him in my possession in the Oseon, you would have lost a valuable 'bot, whereas any poor jerk who took your bait—"

"Precisely. I'm gratified that you appreciate the subtlety of the scheme. That will be all. Officers, take him away."

Lando didn't even have time to protest. The police hauled him from the office, along the corridor, and down a flight of stairs to a waiting hovercruiser. They whisked through the streets to the edge of town, where they entered a forcefence around a series of corrugated-plastic buildings.

"Give him the usual processing," one of the anonymous

visored officers told a fat man in a dirty tunic. "You'll have the paperwork in the morning."

"Very well," the fat man beamed. He was short and greasy looking, but the neuronic whip in one hand and the military blaster in the other added something to his personality. The cruiser roared away.

"Welcome to the penal colony of Rafa IV." The fat man grinned.

Midnight.

Listening to the chanting of the Toka, Lando lay on a steel-slatted cot in a barred cell. Offworld prisoners occupied cells on one side of the corridor; the Toka shared an unlocked kennel-like affair on the other side. Lando was unusual in that the other three bunks in his own cell were unoccupied.

He figured that the governor didn't want him talking to anyone until he was "processed"—whatever that meant.

To say he found the native chanting annoying would have been a calamitous understatement. It was unpleasant enough in itself, but it further served to remind him of Mohs—the little man who wasn't there. If he had been. The question bothered the gambler almost as much as his present predicament did.

More, perhaps, because he'd been in jail before.

Less, perhaps, because he'd never faced a sentence in the life-orchards.

And, unlike the other freshly arrived convicts in the cells around him, he knew what that meant, had had a taste of his mind's being sucked away by the trees from which the crystals were harvested.

And his memories of Mohs were clear; the chanting across the hallway was in no way inconsistent with them. The language was distressingly familiar. He could almost imagine he understood it. Not for the first time, he reasoned that it was a corrupted version of some tongue spoken in a place he'd been once. If only he could remember...

* * *

"ALL RIGHT, RISE AND SHINE!"

The fat man had friends, at least five of them, also armed with blasters and whips. They paced up and down in front of the barred cells, shouting to wake up the offworld prisoners. The Toka were already gone, sometime in the night.

Lando groaned, turned over. Before they'd placed him in the cell, they'd taken his clothes, replacing them with rough-woven pajamas of unbleached cloth. Now he was being ordered to remove even that minimal dress.

He quickly found out why. Two of the guards placed their weapons to one side, manhandled a huge fire hose into place before the cells, and turned it on. Lando was dashed to the back of the cell, where he fetched up against the rough plaster wall and slid to the floor, shielding his eyes against the blast of the water. The stream passed on to the next cell. He rose stiffly, put his shirt back on—he hadn't time to undress all the way before the water hit him—and wondered what came next.

He didn't have to wait long.

"All right, prisoners," the fat man shouted, "we will open the cells in a moment, and you will step outside, stand at attention until told otherwise. Then you will turn left-face and march, single file and silently, into the waiting bus. Step out of line, utter so much as a single word, and you are dead where you stand."

Luckily, Lando didn't have a snappy come-back ready anyway.

The door slid open with a clank. He stepped out and stood stiffly, shivering in the early morning breeze. He had his first look at the compound, and, having looked around, decided he didn't want to make a habit of it. Boxed into the corner between two plastic Sharu buildings hundreds of meters tall and unscalable, the yard was fenced on the other two sides. Bare earth, a handful of small one-story cell blocks, and an administration building. Home sweet home for the rest of his life.

Like hell, Lando swore to himself. He would be free. He had debts to settle.

The command was given. He turned left smartly, walked behind half a dozen other prisoners to the bus, an old one, driven by another convict. Its skirts were stained and tattered. It would be a rough ride this morning. It—

The ground began to shake.

Across the compound, the earth billowed up like waves on the ocean, heaved at the cellblocks, smashing them to bits, ripped the administration building apart, toppled the hoverbus. The man inside it screamed.

Several convicts ran to help the trapped driver. They were shouted at by the guards. One of the uniformed men opened fire, sending a prisoner up in flames that were mirrored by those which suddenly burst from a leaking fuel line in a building on the far side of the yard.

Lando stood where he was, then decided to fall down, since the quake threatened to do it to him anyway, and there was less chance of getting shot. Suddenly, a figure in the town-cop uniform, mirrored helmet visor and all, staggered up to the warden or whatever he was. Lando could hear him over the rumble, roar, and screaming.

"That man is to be turned over for further interrogation!" The armored finger pointed at Lando. The warden and the cop leaned on each other to stay erect.

"I have no authorization! He's mine! Can't this wait?"

"The governor wants him immediately!" There was sudden menace in the big policeman's voice. "Something about a load of cops he tried to maroon on Rafa XI four months ago."

"Then by all means take him. I—" That was all the fat man had to say. He swayed and fell. The cop ducked back, came for Lando.

"Let's go!"

Grabbing Lando by the pajamaed scruff, the cop bore him along toward a waiting cruiser that had been left aground beside the cell block. "Get in!"

They roared away through the gate, which hung open on one hinge. It wouldn't have mattered: the force-fence was down, even its auxiliary power system apparently destroyed in the quake. The car rocked and swayed, turned right, and sped down the road.

"Say, old flatfoot, this isn't the way to Teguta Lusat!" Lando shouted. He cringed as they rounded a corner and dashed toward the country.

"What's it to you? Shut up and mind your own business!"

"Would this make it my business?"

The cop looked down to see what was pressing at his side. It was his own blaster. He raised a visored head to the young gambler.

"Very good. I guess you didn't need rescuing that badly, after all. Want to go back and have all the glory to yourself?"

"What are you talking about?" Lando demanded. "Stop this car and take that helmet off. I want to see who I'm talking to!"

The cruiser slowed as per specification. They halted in the middle of the road and waited out an aftershock. Lando leveled the blaster at the policeman's face. "Okay, take it off."

The gloved hands rose, took the helmet and lifted. In place of a head sticking up through the collar, there was— a *snake*! A chromium-plated snake.

"Can I get out of this uniform, Master? It's very uncomfortable."

"Vuffi Raa! You little—but what's going on here? Why are you rescuing me?"

Shucking the rest of the guardsman's uniform—he'd been walking on two tentacles, using two for arms, and the fifth as an ersatz head—Vuffi Raa assumed a more normal position behind the drive tiller.

"Master, I was programmed to betray you from the beginning, and not to tell you about it. But you're my *Master*, Lando, and, as soon as that program had run out, so did I.

And here I am. We've got to get off this planet, out of the system, and fast."

"I know."

"You know? How?"

"The dreams, the chanting I heard last night. It's Old High Trammic—the language of the Toka. I was on Trammis III a couple of years ago. I still can't understand the language very well, but my subconscious apparently made something of it. I woke up this morning knowing the truth about the Mindharp, and I know we've got to get out of this place *now*."

"Why is that, Master?"

"Don't call me Master. Because, once somebody starts the music up, this system's never going to be the same again."

"Then we must go now, Master. Duttes Mer is using the Harp. That's what the earthquake's all about."

TWENTY

Uɴʟɪᴋᴇ ᴀ ꜰɪᴄᴛɪᴏɴᴀʟ ᴠɪʟʟᴀɪɴ, Dᴜᴛᴛᴇꜱ Mᴇʀ ʜᴀᴅɴ'ᴛ gloated or divulged his plans to the beaten Lando Calrissian. He'd simply had him disposed of, as quickly and neatly as possible.

Where he'd made his mistake—his first one, anyway— was in his attitude toward menials. Toka servants were virtually invisible to him—drinks and cigars simply appeared near his elbow, and that, he thought, was as it should be. He was the governor, after all. Droids were even more invisible.

So Vuffi Raa had stood in plain sight in the governor's office as he made a transspace call to Rokur Gepta.

"Ahhh, it is you, my esteemed sorcerer. I have some news."

"What is it, Mer? It had better be good!"

"Are you enjoying your stay in orbit around a dried-up desert planet?"

"My ship is far more comfortable than that heap of bricks

you call a city. Get on with it, Governor, you're beginning to anger me!"

The governor reached to the pickup on his communicator, pulled it out on a retracting cable, and pointed it at the top of his desk. "See anything you recognize, Gepta?"

In the screen, the sorcerer's eyes were filled, by turn, with wonder, greed, and rage. "The Mindharp! How did you—"

The governor chuckled. "It only matters that I *did*, Gepta, and that you're millions of kilometers from here. You see, that story you told Calrissian—that the Harp is the 'Ultimate Instrument of Music'—may have been good enough for him, but the story you told *me* about its being a master control over all the Toka never washed. Such a thing would be commercially useful, but this," he indicated the Harp, "is much, much more than that."

"What do you mean, Mer?"

"I am capable of hiring investigators, too, my dear former partner, and I took the wisest course: hiring *yours*. Recall that I have the power to commute sentences, order pardons. I know the truth: that the Mindharp of Sharu is an instrument capable of controlling every mind within the system—possibly beyond it. And the instrument is *mine*!"

"Don't try it, Mer, you don't know what you're doing!" Panic was evident in the sorcerer's voice.

"On the contrary, my dear—"

"*NO*! You don't understand! The Mindharp will—"

The governor smiled benignly. "It will give me absolute power, even over you. I suggest that, if you don't want to feel that power, you turn your ship out of orbit and leave my system. That may buy you a few years, at least."

"Mer, I'll warn you once more: you don't have the knowledge to safely—"

Click.

When the opportunity arose—which wasn't until the middle of the night—Vuffi Raa crept from the governor's offices, stole a uniform from the guard laundries, jump-wired a police cruiser in the maintenance yard, and went off to rescue Lando.

"Well, I appreciate it, Vuffi Raa, old criminal, but I trust you'll understand the residue of skepticism that remains within me."

They were whisking back into town at a moderate, legal, and inconspicuous velocity. They had felt several more tremors, but nothing like that first quake.

"I understand," Vuffi Raa acknowledged, "and I suppose telling you I was programmed to betray you is much the same as a human being's saying he couldn't help himself. Well, I came to rescue you by way of restitution."

Lando thought about that. "Very well, and just to show you my good faith, you might as well know that Rokur Gepta and Duttes Mer are *both* wrong about the Mindharp."

Vuffi Raa brought the car to a screeching halt as they neared the outskirts of Teguta Lusat. "What?"

"That's correct. And we've got to get out to the port, steal something that will get us out of the system, but fast."

"Master, I agree about getting out. You don't want your mind controlled, especially by a being like the governor—believe me, I know. But if they're wrong . . ."

"It will be worse, Vuffi Raa. My only regret is leaving the *Falcon* on Rafa V."

"Master, four months have passed. Mer had the *Falcon* brought back. Its cargo of life-crystals hasn't even been unloaded, because until we reappeared in Teguta Lusat, Gupta and Mer didn't know if they might have to bargain more with you."

"What? Why didn't you tell me? He didn't think to have her drives repaired, did he?"

After a long pause, the droid replied, "No, Master, *I* did that, the first thing on the way to Rafa V."

Lando didn't say anything. If he'd realized the extent of the droid's housekeeping back then, they might have taken off and skipped the last four months inside the Sharu ruins.

"Well," he said irritably, "let's get out to the port!"

"Yes, Master."

Aboard the decommissioned cruiser *Wennis*, leaving orbit from Rafa V, a decision had been made. Rokur Gepta lay in a special acceleration couch, being strapped up for the voyage ahead of him. The vessel in the lifeboat bay was not a lifeboat, but an elderly Imperial fighter, refitted as a scout. It could make the trip to Rafa IV in a third the time of its parent vessel.

If the occupant could stand the G-forces involved.

The safety precautions were primarily for the benefit of the crew, Gepta reflected. He didn't need them, but it was dangerous for them to know that. As the last strap and bit of tape was in place and the port clamped down, he relaxed, waited for the tick, and didn't stir a hair when thrust that might have seriously injured a mere human being passed harmlessly through his body.

He'd be in Teguta Lusat within an hour.

Duttes Mer looked down at the Mindharp on his desk, afraid to try again, but desperate to master the weird thing before Gepta could return and take it from him. He had no illusions. If he couldn't control *that* mind, along with millions of others, he was doomed. He placed his short, square hand on the central shaft of the Harp again, suppressed a wave of fear, and tried to concentrate.

"Master!"

Vuffi Raa clung to the steering tiller as the road tried to shake them off its back like a wet dog. Lando grabbed the ends of a seat belt, tried to fasten them together as the police car pitched and swayed.

"This is no good!" he shouted, finally giving up the effort. "Look, let's make a run for it!"

The spaceport gates were only a few hundred meters away, and they were traveling twice that distance weaving back and forth across the road. Lando slammed the door open, rolled out, got to his feet, and ran toward the gate. Vuffi Raa, right behind him, took no time at all to catch up.

A guard, well away from his swaying guardpost, was standing in the gateway. He aimed a blaster at Lando.

"Halt! Looters will be shot!"

"I'm not a looter," Lando hollered as he approached the guard. Both were pretty busily occupied just staying on their feet. "I'm the captain of that ship over there, the *Millennium Falcon*, and I've got to get her off before she breaks up with everything else on this planet!"

The blaster came up to Lando's eye level. "That ship's under the governor's seal. You can't—"

Lando stepped closer. The guard fired, but, swaying as he was, succeeded only in burning a shrub across the road. By that time, Lando was close enough to seize the weapon, push it upward, punch the other man in the solar plexus with his fist.

Flexible armor is for bullets and energy beams. It's no protection at all against an unarmed man. The guard folded. Lando took his gun away, added it to the weapon he'd taken at the labor camp.

"Let's go!"

They ran toward the *Falcon*, and, as they approached it, the boarding ramp swung downward slowly, as if in welcome. Cautiously, Lando and Vuffi Raa walked up the inclined plane.

At the top, still aged and wrinkled, but sporting a stylish haircut and expensive business suit, stood Mohs, High Singer of the Toka. Where his ruined eyes had been now glittered a pair of faceted multicolored optics like those of a giant psychedelic spider.

Duttes Mer glared resentfully at the alien object on his desk. Twice, now, following the mental procedure conveyed to him by Gepta's captive sociologists, he had tried to gain control of the Mindharp, and thus—

He slammed his hand down on the desk, making the object jump. He didn't want to try again; all it seemed to do was cause quakes that threatened to tear his administration building apart. Why that should be, he didn't know, but he knew one thing: Rokur Gepta was coming.

The spaceport radar people had confirmed it, just before the communications lines had gone dead. A small, extremely fast craft was no more than twenty minutes from landfall. Mer suspected that Gepta didn't need the port facilities; there was a wide flat space atop the administration building. It would do nicely for—

He hit the annunciator button. "Give me the Captain of the Guard!"

At first there was no answer. Then a terrified secretary told him, "Sir, the guard contingent has left the building because of the tremors. I was about to go, myself. I—"

"If you leave, I'll have you shot. Summon those four men who went to Rafa XI. They're under house arrest here in the building. Tell them to get up on the roof and—never mind, I'll tell them myself!"

Once more, he looked upon the Mindharp. It had better work this time.

Rokur Gepta was coming.

"You will pardon my dramatic appearance, Captain Calrissian," Mohs said as he ushered them around the curving corridor toward the *Falcon*'s cockpit, "but things are beginning to happen, and I am too busy to be anything *but* dramatic."

"I know," Lando said, throwing himself into the left-hand seat. He flipped a couple of switches and helped Vuffi Raa through the preflight checklist. It was a long list, much too long for comfort. "I know everything—but I'm in something of a hurry myself right now."

Mohs looked puzzled, then relaxed and grinned. "Ah, yes. You put the pieces together. All my life I was the instrument of my ancestors, given orders—the Voices of the Gods—whisked thither and yon at Their bidding. It was terrifying to the savage that I was, for example, to brush near an ancient wall, as I did that night in Teguta Lusat, and appear an instant later, leagues away, amidst a gathering of my people. I apologize also for vanishing from the tunnel; its purpose was elementary education, you see, and I matriculated and went on to higher things." He absently ran a fingertip over his bizarre eyes. "The decision was made *for* me, and I—"

"Had no choice about it?" Lando asked. He looked at Vuffi Raa. "There's a lot of that going around. What in heaven's name is that red light on the life-support panel! Here, let's override—"

"You are in no danger," Mohs smiled. "The two of you helped me, and now I shall help you. We mean you no harm."

"Swell. Can you fend off the governor and his friend the sorcerer?"

"I can tell you that the governor is alone, trying to use the Mindharp, while Gepta is on his way from Rafa V. He ought to be down any minute, but he won't be coming to the spaceport."

Lando turned to look at the old man, no longer bent and wizened. He was still old, but it lent him dignity and authority now.

The tattoo of the Key—the Mindharp, Lando realized—was darker now, stood out more sharply on the old man's forehead. It practically glowed.

"Are there any more like you?" Lando asked.

"No, Captain, I am the only one. I am all there ever was, of *my* generation. The burden was to be passed on next year, but here I am."

"Master, what are you talking about?"

"Quiet, Vuffi Raa. Watch the temperature in that reactor!"

"I assure you, Captain, everything is under control. You'd realize that, if you truly know our secrets."

"I *know* your secrets, Mohs, believe me. There never were any pre-Republican colonists here, right?"

"That is correct, Captain."

"But what are you saying, Master? If—"

"Nor were there really any Toka. Or would that be telling?"

"Master—"

"*Quiet!* You people *are* the Sharu. It's written all over your walls inside the pyramid. You're humanoid and very, very advanced. I don't know what scared you into this masquerade—and I'm willing to bet you don't either!"

"Master, will you please explain—"

"All right, all right. Mohs will correct me over the rough spots. I hardly understand contemporary Trammic, let alone an ancient—and thoroughly synthetic—version. But this is the gist: something pretty scary threatened the Sharu. Something that liked to eat hyperadvanced cultures but that wouldn't bother with savages.

"So, a vast computer system was created. That's all the so-called ruins in the system. The Sharu, before the threat, lived in cities not terribly different from our own, and they're probably concealed beneath the monumental architecture, too—along with the *intelligence* of the Sharu. Hand me that checklist a moment."

"Very good, Captain, very good."

"You bet it's good. The life-orchards weren't created to increase intelligence or longevity. They were created to suck it away from the population. I'll bet three-quarters of everybody's mind on the planet is stored inside that pyramid and other buildings like it. That's so succeeding generations would be disguised as savages, too. But, when the crystals were separated from the trees by the colonists, the things absorbed small amounts of intelligence and life-force from the ambient environment, then fed them back to whoever wore the crystal—an accidental and unlooked-for effect."

The old man nodded. "The colonists' harvesting did no harm. What was of real value was stored in the buildings."

"The buildings," Lando continued, "may be the biggest computer system ever created. When this colony was founded, the computer searched our records, came up with a missing pre-Republican colony ship, and decided to use that as a cover story. The Sharu—reduced to mere Toka-hood—were poor savage brutes, 'broken' by their experience with the mighty Sharu.

"I just couldn't swallow it. What were the Sharu afraid of? How could they be so mighty, and yet—"

"I still don't know the answer to that, Captain. It was expunged from the records, out of sheer terror, I think. It worries me."

"It ought to. Ready, Vuffi Raa?"

"I think so, Master. Yes, we're ready."

Another tremor rocked the ship.

"Mer's trying to use the Harp again. Boy, will he be disappointed. It's a trap, isn't it, Mohs?"

"I'm afraid so," the old man admitted gravely. "The legends were spread among my people in order to entice members of another intelligent species into finding and using the Harp. That way, we'd know that it was safe to come out of hiding."

"Your giant computer system will regurgitate all those smarts it's been storing for thousands of years, the covers will be stripped off your cities—there's going to be a good deal of earth-moving around here, isn't there?"

"All over the system."

"And when the dust clears, the Sharu will be back in control. Well, considering the governor and the nature of the colony here, it can't happen too soon for me. We're leaving. Better jump off, Mohs. I'd say it's been nice to know you, but I hate being used, by governors, sorcerers, or representatives of semilost civilizations."

* * *

Rokur Gepta swept down upon the governor's office building. As he'd expected, guards were posted all over the miniature landing field.

He cleared them away with a burst of the craft's blasters and set down lightly amid the smoking remains. The ground trembled again, and this time it didn't stop. Gepta hurried down to the penthouse office.

He thrust the doors aside and walked into a burst of radiance. Gepta was thrown against the corridor wall as energy streamed out all around him. He squinted his eyes, employed certain other protections, and gazed briefly at the governor's desk.

The Mindharp of Sharu shone far too bright to be looked upon, even by the sorcerer. Behind it, his fat hands wrapped around the base, stood the governor, his mouth and eyes opened wide, frozen, paralyzed.

And doomed.

Even as Gepta watched, both governor and Harp began to melt, to fuse, showering the room and hall with deadly radiation. He regained his feet and ran back up as the earth tremors redoubled.

It was a scene from hell. All around, as far as the horizon, the giant forms left by the Sharu were shifting, fusing, melting like the Harp or, occasionally, detonating rather spectacularly. Something else was rising from the rubble, something Gepta didn't want to see.

He leaped into his scoutship but nearly tumbled it off the roof before he got it properly airborne. Ahead, toward the spaceport, an ungainly crustacean-shaped object lifted from the runway.

Gepta cursed.

He heeled the fighter around, then aimed it straight for the *Millennium Falcon*. Closing, closing, he laid a thumb on the firing stud, his crosshairs on the unsuspecting freighter.

Two things happened.

Aboard the *Falcon*, another thumb rode another stud. Energy streaked toward the fighter Vuffi Raa had noticed landing on the roof. The *Falcon*'s radar was good, and they'd both been alert against flying debris.

I may not be much of a pilot yet, but I can shoot, Lando thought.

Almost simultaneously, a small obelisk of Sharu manufacture exploded beneath Gepta's fighter, driving fragments into the small craft. The explosion staggered the scout, disabling it but throwing it from the path of Lando's beam.

Seconds later, Rokur Gepta clambered from the wreckage as the *Millennium Falcon* soared away, safe, and with a precious load: the last life-crystals ever to be harvested in the Rafa System. Lando would be very, very rich.

Gepta shook a fist at the departing ship.

Someday . . .

ABOUT THE AUTHOR

Self-defense consultant and former police reservist, L. Neil Smith has also worked as a gunsmith and a professional musician. Born in Denver in 1946, he traveled widely as an Air Force "brat," growing up in a dozen regions of the United States and Canada. In 1964, he returned home to study philosophy, psychology, and anthropology, and wound up with what he refers to as perhaps the lowest grade-point average in the history of Colorado State University.

L. Neil Smith's previous books—all published by Ballantine/Del Rey—are *The Probability Broach, The Venus Belt, Their Majesties' Bucketeers,* and *The Nagasaki Vector.*